Cigar City Crimes,
Triple Jeopardy

Cigar City Crimes

Triple Jeopardy

BOOK TWO IN THE
KYLE McNALLY DETECTIVE SERIES

J. E. BOYDSTON

and M. BROOKE McCULLOUGH

Cigar City Crimes, Triple Jeopardy
Book Two in the Kyle McNally Detective Series

Copyright © 2025 by J. E. Boydston and M. Brooke McCullough

Cigar City Crimes is a work of fiction. Names, characters, places, and incidents either are products of the authors' imaginations or are used fictitiously. Any resemblance to actual persons, living or dead, or events, is entirely coincidental.

Interior formatting by Alt 19 Creative

ISBN 979-8-9929520-0-1 (Paperback)
ISBN 979-8-9929520-1-8 (Digital)
ISBN 979-8-9929520-2-5 (Hardback)

Published by:
Canarytown LLC

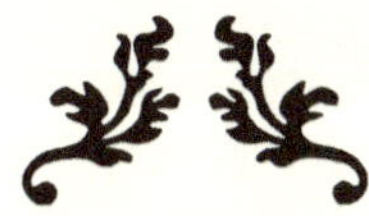

ACKNOWLEDGMENTS

First, this novel wouldn't be possible without the guidance and careful attention to detail of my sister, Brooke. Her deep knowledge of criminology and police procedures has been a godsend for me. Thanks, Sis! *It's on to Book Three now.*

Other critical assistance has been rendered by my dauntless beta readers, including Robert Louty, Cindy Morris-Marrs, Mary Ann Trenary, John Chaplick, the one who keeps me grounded in the *art* of prose, Ratna and Christopher Scherrer, Denise Michele Simsek, Gayle Wolfe, Sylvia Crim, and Steven Palukaitis.

I am also deeply indebted to my buddy, Ron Ludwin, and to Matthew Gorecki for their invaluable assistance in advising and reviewing the opening sniper scene. You both helped to make it 'frosty.'

A final nod to the University of North Florida, Thomas G. Carpenter Library, Special Collections and Archives Department for their generous permission to use the image of the Simovitz Building in Ybor City, Tampa, FL.

J. E. Boydston

In memory of my friend, Ronaldus Maximus.

*"I know that pain is the most important thing in
the universes. Greater than survival, greater than
love, greater even than the beauty it brings about.
For without pain, there can be no pleasure. Without
sadness, there can be no happiness. Without misery
there can be no beauty. And without these, life is
endless, hopeless, doomed and damned."*
—Harlan Ellison

"Carpe Diem"
— Horace

"Memento Mori"
— Anonymous

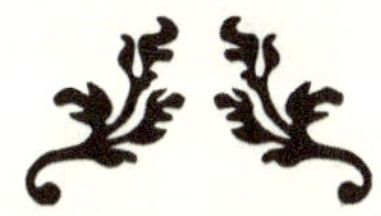

PROLOGUE

NOVEMBER 5, 1999

11:15:00 — I drive my white Ford Econoline Van to the top, thirteenth floor of the parking garage on North Tampa Street. The driver's door logo implies I work with the Ballistic Services Company. From my earlier reconnaissance, I choose the last two spaces on the northeast corner, a location bounded by a high wall to the east and a three-foot wall to the north. This gives me shielding from the right, and a unobstructed view north toward downtown Tampa. Today I have a thick beard and dark reflective sunglasses. I'm wearing loose-fitting jeans, a long-sleeved Tampa Bay Lightning sweatshirt with an embroidered Vinny Lecavalier signature, and a reflective orange vest. I complete my disguise with a yellow construction hard hat and scuffed-up Timberland work boots. There are the distinct aromas of fried chicken, French fries, chili powder, and cumin drifting up from food trucks on the streets below.

11:18:02 — I unload four orange traffic cones, three six-foot tall sections of stand-up steel framing, and enough black Visqueen to provide perimeter cover. After assembling the frames, I clip the Visqueen in place and position the cones. I remove a folding platform and a drag bag containing the rest of my *tools* from the van. Elapsed time: 14 minutes, 06 seconds.

11:32:08 — I assemble my shooting platform and rifle support tripod, placing them in position four feet back from the low wall. I outfit an M24 Remington Sniper Rifle, my favorite I nicknamed *Dire Fate,* with five steel-jacketed Winchester .338 Magnum cartridges in the internal magazine, confident I'll only need one. I complete my weapon assembly by mounting a Leupold Mark4 LR/T 10x40 Tactical Sniper Scope and Dark Earth Sound Suppressor. Elapsed time: 10 minutes, 12 seconds.

11:42:20 — Every aspect and every outcome commands my attention. The weather is perfect with moderate humidity and nominal wind. The air temperature is a cool sixty-eight degrees. At midday, this time of year, the sun's location is more southerly, placing it behind me and lighting my target. I took several weeks confirming the man always takes his Friday lunches at the Cigar City Pizza Parlor. I calculate the distance to be two hundred ten meters from my firing position. The target regularly enters by, or shortly before 12:00 p.m., and leaves within a minute or two of 12:45 p.m. I settle into my ready position. My plan: take him as he leaves the restaurant.

12:47:28 — Ninety-two minutes after parking, I execute my long-practiced military pre-shot checklist. Finger resting on trigger, I confirm a clear field of fire when, on this particular Friday, at exactly 12:47:50, my target exits the restaurant and stops directly behind a woman waiting for a traffic signal. She's waving to someone across the street. I couldn't chance waiting for a better shot. I take it. They both collapse to the sidewalk.

12:48:06 — After a moment's hesitation by those closest to the fallen victims, the reality of the situation crashes home. Panicking people begin screaming and scrambling in all directions. I anticipated this pandemonium; confident it would delay a quick response by authorities.

13:02:22 — I pack my tools, remove the curtains and frames, stow the cones, and sweep any evidence of my presence in the garage. Pulling out of the parking space, the only reminder of my being there is a vague smell of burnt gunpowder. I pull a Tampa Bay Lightning ball cap over my forehead and drive out, turning south on Tampa Street. With my window down, the first responders' earsplitting horns compete with the pulsating screams of the police sirens. Checking my side-view mirror, I smile, pleased with the mayhem on the street three blocks behind me, as the radio plays Queen's *Who Wants To Live Forever*.

CHAPTER 1

OCTOBER 28, 1999
(EIGHT DAYS EARLIER)

THE NATIONAL HURRICANE Center issued a tropical storm warning threatening the eastern Caribbean islands and Florida. It was on a track forecast to hit the Cayman Islands, Cuba, and south Florida. The season had already been brutal, with three category three and four storms. They named this one Marcos. Current forecast tracks showed it passing south and east of Tampa, but one had it barreling right up I-75. Currently, NHC predicted the storm, with sustained winds of sixty knots, was likely to progress to category three once past Cuba.

DETECTIVE KYLE MCNALLY sat on the condominium patio, holding the hand of his fiancée, Dr. Mykel Hartley. Their home offered a beautiful view of the Hillsborough River, the Tampa Bay Performing Arts Center, a burgeoning downtown skyline, and the University of Tampa's distinctive silver-topped Arabian minarets. At times like these, Kyle took the

1

world off his shoulders for a few hours. And so far, no sign of Marcos on the horizon.

"I'm sure fate had a hand in the good fortune that's come our way, Kyle. I've never been happier or felt safer," Mykel said.

"That was my promise. And, two weeks from now we'll both be marrying our best friend. Sitting here beside you, with the glistening minarets across the river, I can't deny the faith ancient Arabians held in fatalism; but whether it's fate, fortune, or karma, my love, carpe diem, right?"

Mykel smiled and dabbed at the tears welling up from her sparkling azure-blue eyes, and said, "I confirmed our wedding plans with the pastor at the Unitarian Church today. When we visited, we loved the idyllic country setting, the charming arched chapel surrounded by old live oak trees. I gave him our small guest list, including your father Patrick, our friends Tony, Leo and his wife, Camille."

"I've thought about that honey, and I think we should invite our friends Guillermo and his sister Rosalina from the restaurant."

"I sorry I overlooked them. Remind me to bring an invitation in the morning."

THEIR MOVE TO Tampa, Florida in early 1998, was the perfect choice. Kyle and Mykel planned it for nearly a year. She'd settled in peacefully since the trauma Francis Butler, aka the Slugger, triggered two years before. His brutal attack nearly killed her. She took comfort knowing he'd spend the rest of his life looking through windows barred with metal grates at Chicago-Read Hospital.

They pooled their savings to buy the condominium and a deck boat, moored at a slip on the river minutes from their home. She loved her position at Tampa General Hospital as a Medical Pathologist. Kyle opened his private investigation firm, Paladin Detective Agency, on 7th Avenue in nearby Ybor City.

This was another one of many peaceful evenings spent here on the balcony, sharing a bottle of wine, enjoying classical music.

"Can this last forever, Kyle?" Mykel said.

"I'm certain of it. And honey, together, forever will be a long, wonderful time," Kyle replied, raising his glass to hers.

CHAPTER 2

OCTOBER 29, 1999
(SEVEN DAYS EARLIER)

KYLE AND MYKEL met outside the Sagua La Grande Cantina in Ybor City for breakfast. The owner, Guillermo Posada, befriended him soon after Kyle opened his agency on 7th Avenue. The restaurant was two blocks south on 5th Avenue.

The air inside the restaurant was thick with the nutty, chocolatey fragrance of coffee and fresh buttered Cuban bread toasting. While they waited to be seated, Mykel said, "I enjoyed the story Guillermo told of having bribed a high-ranking agent at the Cuban Embassy. He won Rosalina's visa by serving the pliable bureaucrat lavish dinners for a full week. Shortly after, she was flying to the States. She'd recently escaped a toxic marriage from a loathsome, abusive man, a man Guillermo never approved of."

Kyle nodded. "He's very protective of his younger sister. He arranged for Rosa to attend American schools growing up. He wanted her to have the advantages he didn't. They grew up in Sagua La Grande, Cuba, namesake of the restaurant."

The cantina was a crowded, noisy place during breakfast and lunch hours, with plates clattering and orders being called out. It also had a small private room off the main dining area where friends of Guillermo were invited to sit.

This morning, Guillermo, a slender man with skin the color of the coffee he brewed, a thick mustache, and a full head of dusty brown hair, greeted the two of them with his characteristic generous, smile. "Hola mis amigos, how are you both on this wonderful morning?"

"Couldn't be better today, Guillermo. Mykel and I are here for your Cuban toast with ham and cheese, and Cafe con Leche."

"Hi Guillermo. So good to see you," Mykel said. "If you have a moment, could you answer a question that's interested me for some time?"

"Si, with pleasure," he answered, with a sparkle in his eyes.

"I've always admired the lovely wall murals on your walls, but never asked you about them. They must be special. Please tell me about them."

"It would make me happy to," he replied, gesturing toward the one in the main dining room. "This one show two lovers dancing and kissing. I name it Bolero, *the Dance of Love*. In Cuba, young people who are in love don't go to a movie to be together. They stay home with family and dance all night. And, here," he said, walking them into the Guadalupe Room, "is the bridge over the Sagua La Grande river, in the town where I come from." Then, with a chuckle, "The name mean big mouse.

"Please, sit here where you can talk quietly. Now that you show interest, the name of this room, Guadalupe, mean *valley of the wolf.* A wolf is very protective of his family pack. But now, let me put in your order and have Rosa bring your coffee."

"Have you heard the weather reports?" Kyle said.

"Sí. That storm hit Cuba next. I am sorry now for them."

"Marcos might hit us early next week. I read the last time was the Tampa Bay Hurricane eighty years ago. They said it was a Category four."

Guillermo was shaking his head, rubbing the back of his neck and said, "This is a storm that worry us all. I never see one in this city, but in Cuba, there were many. They are the angry face of Yemaya; Marcos mean 'go to war' in my language. I pray for the good people of my home country."

"They got the name right," Mykel said. "I'll be praying too.

"Guillermo, Kyle and I have brought an invitation for Rosa and you. We're hoping you'll both come to our wedding in two weeks on the thirteenth."

"This is very exciting! I must tell Rosa. Of course we will join you."

Rosa delivered their coffees. "Hello, Mykel. It's always nice to have you both here together. And Kyle, you *do* realize she's truly your better half," she said with a grin and a wink at Mykel. "I'm bringing you both a special coffee this morning. It's one we only offer when Guillermo is occasionally inspired. It's called Cortadito, and is a Cuban specialty that requires more elaborate preparation than the traditional Cuban Café. I guarantee you'll both love it."

Mykel admired Rosa: *She is a tall, attractive woman who looks ten years younger than her age. Her complexion is lighter than her brother's, and she wears makeup sparingly—but doesn't suffer for it. With a shapely figure and dazzling, raven-black hair, tied back, down to her waist, Mykel was stumped trying to imagine how Rosa remained single, being well past her first 'bad' marriage. And, the woman could keep her cool, even when the staff were overwhelmed, and 'in the weeds.' She's proud, but not haughty; statuesque, and walks through the cantina like every step is intentional. She'd be a good find for any man.*

Rosalina's eyes sparkled as she said, "Guillermo tells me you've invited us to your wedding. I'm so excited for you two! We'll be there. It's such a happy time and a perfect occasion to be shared with friends and family. Thank you for asking us." Then she paused, smiled, and said, "I've spoken with Guillermo. You must allow us to provide food for your reception."

"Oh please, we're just happy you're both coming Rosa. And, though I appreciate your kind offer, we'd never want to impose on you, but thank you for asking," Mykel said.

"No no, you're mistaken. It will be our honor Mykel. Our gift to you both. It's no imposition. Let's get together and decide on your menu."

THEIR BREAKFAST FINISHED, they discussed plans for the weekend. Kyle said, "There's a new exhibit opening at the Dali Museum today. They're displaying surrealists from the 1930's and 40's. How about we take the Floribbean Flow over there tomorrow, stop for lunch at The Landing, and walk to the exhibition?"

"I'm in. And after, while we're in the neighborhood, let's swing by the outdoor market for veggies and fruit on our way home. I'll need one of those gigantic eggplants they sell. I'm dying for your eggplant parmigiana."

"I hope that's not all you've been *craving* lately," he said, leaning over, leaving a tender peck on her cheek. "So it's a date. And on Monday, I've invited Patrick over for drinks and dinner. It'll be a good time to discuss the preparations for our wedding."

"Good, that'll also give us a chance to clarify *our* plans for *our* ceremony. He's disappointed that we're not marrying in a Catholic church. As much as he'd like it, I refuse to consider changing my faith."

Leaving the restaurant, Kyle noticed men on a lumber truck unloading four-foot by eight-foot sheets of plywood at the business next door.

CHAPTER 3

OCTOBER 30TH, 1999
(SIX DAYS EARLIER)

THE BLACK DRAGON Security Solutions Company was holding a Saturday morning meeting in the conference room on the 10th floor of the downtown Franklin Building. Present were the owner and CEO, Dominic Papadapolis, his partner Felix Hermann, Vice President of Marketing, and Scott Kaine, their Lead Programmer and Technical Support Manager.

"You're here today, because our Year 2000, or 'Y2K', software issues appear to have stalled. Given our position as an industry leader in cybersecurity, it's hard for me to believe we're at risk. With only two months until the so-called millennial meltdown, we by God better get these problems resolved, and I mean immediately," Papadapolis said, nostrils flaring.

"Scott, give me your worst-case sitrep on my software's Y2K compliance worldwide."

"We're okay domestically, Mr. P, but there's several of our middle and far eastern customers who've fallen behind. I've been pushing them to fix their programs, but in those regions, I don't see any way they'll get it done by the new year unless someone lights a fire under their asses.

"I tell ya, I'm about as optimistic as a blind-folded man in front of a firing squad, Mr. P. First, the original programs you purchased, the ones I adapted, were written using the COBOL language. Locating competent coders in the U.S. is a challenge, but it's ten times tougher overseas. Second, the coding they *are* doing is sloppy. Despite several attempts, I can't seem to get those Arab and Cossack code jockeys on top of it. The worst offenders work at our Saudi and Russian sites. They believe shitty programming is somehow akin to epic poetry."

With a clamped jaw, and staring straight at Kaine, Papadapolis began rapping his pen on the table.

Kaine continued, "Trust me, it'd freak you out how many times I've caught them taking idiotic shortcuts ending with calculation errors, BSODs, and system crashes at those sites. I've tried everything to get them off their asses; but it's like trying to teach seals to string a Stradivarius. If they can't get it right before January first, those businesses will hit the shitter, and drag us down with them."

Perspiration beads shining on his forehead, he glanced back and forth at the faces of the men seated with him. "Y2K isn't just a problem for us. It's real and it's gonna be big. I've talked with a dozen IT shops and they all shared panic and doomsday forecasts with me, sir."

Felix Hermann leaned forward. "So tell us, Scott, what do we do to make sure this doesn't become a marketing problem for me? Do you need more help? We'll get it if it'll help."

"No, thanks though, Mr. H. I'll give you a list of those shops that have to fix their code so you two can put the fear of Beelzebub in their bosses. That'll help. They've all got my list of necessary corrections. Sadly, I suspect there's a greater than a twenty percent chance I'll be putting out fires well into January. Not exactly what I'd call a winning movie script, is it?"

One final time, Papadapolis rapped his pen loudly on the table and said, "No, and I agree. Meantime, bring us your list of those trouble sites.

"Oh, and Kaine, are we prepared in case Hurricane Marcos tracks here to Tampa? It's a Cat 3 now, passing Cuba, and at least one of the tracks shows it making it here."

"You bet Mr. P, all our hurricane preps are in place; sandbags are ready, the generator is gassed up, and we have backups secured off-site, so there's nothing to worry about."

"Good. That's all for now. Wait in your office while Felix and I decide our next move."

Scott nodded. "Yes sir."

FELIX SHOOK HIS head. "Dominic, right from the start, you gave our customers management and control of their own software updates and maintenance. That move led to a trend, and it's now industry standard. But we're competing with the largest players in the cybersecurity marketplace, and, as the frontrunner, we can't afford to fail. Frankly, I'm worried. Have you got any ideas how we resolve it before January 1st?"

"That's why we're here, Felix."

"And, let me ask, do you completely trust Kaine's judgement about the extent of the problem? Lately he's been behaving oddly. I don't need to speak of his recent *interesting* wardrobe choices: that gaudy turban hat and parachute pants. Not exactly business appropriate, is it? And, the number of times I've passed his vacant office during business hours seems like a problem needing a fix. Do you agree?

Dom nodded. "Yes Felix, but I'm confident he's okay. He's told me he broke up recently with his longtime girlfriend. I suspect maybe that, and the pressure from this Y2K thing, is taking a toll on his normally dependable performance." Then, adjusting his tie, "But don't worry, I'm keeping a close eye on him.

"Back to the Y2K problem, it's imperative for us to visit these troubled customer sites and notify them how serious this is. If they balk, we need to threaten them. If they don't meet our Y2K standards by January first, I'll cutoff their usage of, and support for, my Dragon Security Software suite. At that point, if it comes to it, I'll eat the losses!

"So Felix, here's what I need you to do: be prepared to travel Monday. I'm sending you to my Arabian accounts in Riyadh. Make the arrangements and forward your itinerary to me by this afternoon. When you return, we'll talk before I fly to Moscow to meet with my Russian accounts there."

His face twisted for a split-second before barking, "You *will* be ready to go by Monday, right, Felix?" Dom barked.

CHAPTER 4

NOVEMBER 1, 1999
(FOUR DAYS EARLIER)

GLANCING SKYWARD AS Kyle grabbed the mail from the box downstairs, there was an ominous line of black clouds moving in from the south. Marcos was now a Cat 4 storm, stalled 200 miles south of Tampa and threatening landfall at Naples. It had practically flattened George Town in the Caymans, and left a devastating trail through Cuba, passing just west of Havana. NOAA forecasters still had one odious path heading directly for Tampa.

Tampa earned its "Cigar City" nickname due to a surge of immigrants from Cuba, Spain, Italy, and Germany in the late 1800s and early 1900s. Vicente Martinez Ybor, a Cuban cigar maker and factory owner, was one of the first to settle here. Over the following decades, the cigar industry boomed, with over 100 factories producing millions of cigars each year.

A number of distinct social clubs—El Centro Español, El Centro Asturiano, La Unión Martí-Maceo, and the Deutscher-Americaner Club—were built to serve the factories' newly-arriving workforce. Though most of the factories were now closed, their unique architectures contributed to the growing gentrification of Ybor's neighborhoods. Kyle appreciated the Cuban influenced ambience and pace of the area, including the near-constant presence of roosters and hens wandering the streets.

He walked into the offices of the Paladin Detective Agency on the 2nd floor of the historic Simovitz building on East 7th Avenue. The four rooms included a large reception area, two offices with doorways to outdoor, over-the-sidewalk balconies, and arch-topped windows.

Mykel had decorated the offices and suggested, "You'll need wall-to-wall carpeting for warmth, period art reflecting Ybor's historic Cigar City past, and sturdy, comfortable Craftsman furniture."

Kyle would have been content with bare wood floors, metal desks and steel file cabinets—*bulletproof stuff*. As he surveyed the offices, the only thing missing was a receptionist/office manager. The fast-growing business would require him to initiate that hire soon.

Stepping out on his balcony, the sky had gone slate gray, and the wind began whipping in intermittent blasts out of the south. The ringing phone drew him back to his office.

"Paladin Detective Agency, Kyle McNally speaking."

The caller hesitated briefly before speaking. "Uh. Oh. Hello. I'm sorry, but I expected an answering machine. They're so damn common these days. I guess I've come to expect them," the caller said in an impatient tone.

"I'm happy to surprise you, ma'am. How can I help you?" Kyle said.

"My name is Jolene Papadapolis, and I need to hire a private detective to find the people who want to kill me."

"Kill you? That's a serious accusation. Have you gone to the police for help yet?"

"Yes, I've spoken with them. They aren't taking me seriously; even after I got run off the road last week on Bayshore. They suggested the accident was my fault since I'd had a couple of cocktails. But that's not true. I was in perfect control of my vehicle."

Kyle opened a new case folder and began taking notes. "Ms. Papadapolis, please give me the date and time of the accident. I'll follow-up with the police."

"It happened last Saturday night, the thirtieth, at around eight o'clock. I'm driving south on Bayshore Boulevard, and a car pulls beside me and cuts right into me. It was me or him and I wasn't in any mood to play chicken, so I swerved off of the road, right into a tree."

"Did you recognize the driver? Were there any passengers in the car?"

"No, it was dark. I was startled and afraid. Can't say I got a good look at them.

"Did you require any medical attention?"

"No."

"Are there other reasons you suspect your life may be in danger?"

"Well, yes there are. I've been followed the past few weeks. It's never the same person, someone different every time I spot them."

"Did you recognize any of these stalkers?"

"No. Don't know any of them. But believe me, Mr. McNally, my life is in danger and I need your help."

"Did the police file a report?"

"Oh sure. No word back from them though. From the way they talked, I'd bet my report ended up in their litter box."

"Have you spoken with anyone else about the stalking?"

"Yeah, my husband Dominic. But he says I'm probably imagining the whole thing. He rarely takes me seriously."

"Even so, I'd like to talk with him. He may have some useful information. Would it be alright if I contact him?"

"Yeah, I suppose so."

Inspecting his haphazardly notated schedule book, Kyle said, "Good. Mrs. Papadapolis, the earliest I'm available is tomorrow afternoon. That's assuming Hurricane Marcos doesn't change course and head this way. If we can't make it then, I'll schedule another day."

"No, no no. I'll be there; to hell with the weather," she said with a nervous chuckle. "I don't want to spend one more day in fear. Thank you, Mr. McNally. I feel better already. And please, call me Jo."

"Alright Jo. I'll look for you tomorrow at two."

CHAPTER 5

NOVEMBER 1, 1999
(FOUR DAYS EARLIER)

PATRICK MCNALLY, KYLE'S step-father and retired Interpol investigator, hung his dripping jacket on a hall tree by the door. Arms spread wide and, on her tiptoes, Mykel greeted him giving him a hug. "Hello Patrick, it's so good to see you. Please tell Kyle and I all about your trip back home to Ireland last month. I hope your time there provided you with many good days for drying," she punctuated with a wink.

"Aye lass, I enjoyed many a fine day. It was good to get back over the pond and reconnect with some of the lads from my years at Interpol. Had a first-rate time with them, though 'tween you and me, I'm of the opinion that most of them have become flippin' eejits. They're all either divorced and pretending they're twenty-one again, or they spend their days at Fairyhouse Racecourse bettin' the ponies. Some sad lot they've become. Don't get me wrong, I still love 'em, but I can't be hangin' around all day drinkin' stout in the pubs like I used to."

With a bemused smile, Mykel said, "So are you ready for our big day? Our wedding is on the 13th, a week from Saturday."

For a second, the creases around Patrick's eyes deepened. *The thirteenth. Now there's a fateful date.* Then, shaking his head, "Don't you worry lass, I'll not be forgettin' it."

Kyle entered the room with cocktails.

Turning to Kyle, Patrick continued. "Son, this is truly the best idea you've had in years. Mykel's sure a real sharp gal. You got lucky with this bonnie lass, my boy! Let me offer a toast to both yours and Mykel's future happiness." As they tipped their glasses, he continued, *"Bíodh airgead i do phóca agat i gcónaí, bean mhaith le grá, agus aoibh gháire ar d'aghaidh."*

Kyle caught Mykel's puzzled expression, and explained, "It's an Irish toast. It loosely translates to, 'May you always have money in your pocket, a good woman to love, and a smile on your face.'"

"What a lovely sentiment. Thank you, Patrick," Mykel said.

"I'm certainly hoping that nasty bit of weather, Marcos, they're callin' it, doesn't ruin your plans for the wedding."

"It's now a Cat 4. Winds up to 130 knots. We should know in the next day or two if we need to change plans," Kyle said.

"Right now, I'm sayin' prayers that doesn't come to pass."

They sat and chatted for another hour, with Patrick sharing tales from his visit back home, when Kyle looked at Mykel and said, "Our reservations at the Columbia Restaurant are in an hour. If you need to get ready, this would be a good time."

Kyle joined Mykel in the bedroom. "We haven't really talked about our wedding plans with Patrick yet. Do you want me to bring it up, or would you prefer to?"

"Let's play it by ear."

Sounding like a distant locomotive engine's horn, the wind whistled through their balcony screens, and the sky overhead took on an eerie shade of green. Hurricane Marcos was blowing up the skirt of the Cigar City.

SEATED AT THE restaurant, their waitress came to the table and stood beside Kyle. Resting a hand on his shoulder, she said, "Good evening, friends. Welcome to the Columbia Restaurant. My name is Carmen, and I'll be your server tonight." Bending down and speaking directly to Kyle, she asked, "And for you, sir, what may I bring?"

"Thank you, Carmen, tonight we'll start with a bottle of your Monte Real Gran Reserva."

Carmen made note of his order, then smiled broadly, "As you wish, Señor!"

After Carmen left, Mykel grinned playfully, "It looks like the McNally charm is still ringing the ladies' bells, Kyle—another reminder of how fortunate I am."

"You never need to worry about my love, Mykel."

With the meal orders placed, wine opened, glasses poured, and toasts made, Mykel bit her lip before speaking. "Patrick, Kyle and I want to discuss our decision to marry in the Unitarian Church. We're well aware you'd prefer a Catholic ceremony."

"Tell me again why you're not havin' your vows consecrated by a priest in the Holy Catholic Church."

Kyle took Mykel's hand as she replied. "We made our choice knowing that God isn't present in only one faith or in one church. We believe in a divine being, but we're not committed to the sacred traditions of your church. We'll follow the bible's teachings, but we agree the Catholic scriptures aren't the only path to spiritual grace."

Kyle nodded with a faint smile as he said, "The Unitarian church where we're marrying is open to people of all denominations. They make no demands on a strict adherence to a single doctrine, or rigorous rules and the ceremonial rites of your church."

Patrick's eyes widened. "Not Catholic? Tis' sad. But, given you two agree, I'd be a sore fool to fuss more about it. May God's blessings be on both of you."

The waitress returned with their appetizers. Patrick smiled and raised both hands in submission, signaling the conversation needed no further discussion. *May the good Lord help them. Among their choice of church, the inauspicious date of the ceremony, and Hurricane Marcos, I hope this doesn't end up a bad dose for the two of them.*

Second Horsman's Arrived!
World That Was Now Crashes Down.
Your People IT's Failed...
Don't Guess Who I Am, Just Ask.

\- Y2K

CHAPTER 6

IT WAS JUST after nine p.m. when I park on the street that fronts DeSoto Park in south Ybor. I roll down my window, kill the headlights, and turn off the engine. Though Hurricane Marcos was still hours away, the air is sopping wet. Its outer bands noisily rustle nearby Cabbage Palm fronds. The odor coming from the bay waters beside the park combined with the atmosphere leaves a musty, moldy stench in my nose.

I sit for several minutes, waiting. I'd stopped a hundred feet in front of the lone, late-night pedestrian. He moves with a noticeable hitch in his gait and struggles with a two-wheeled grocery cart. Under the dim lighting of antique street lamps, He's wearing a ski cap and multiple sweatshirts, the top one imprinted with 'Just Do It,' and a swoop. How ironic, I recall the fabled origin of the corporate motto *Nike* adopted. When the prison guards asked double murderer Gary Gilmore if he had any last words before facing his firing squad, he answered, 'Let's do it.' I always admired Gilmore's style, his gutsy acceptance of death, and the poetic genius I found in his verse, '*The Land Lord.*'

When the homeless man hobbles to within twenty feet of the car, I get out and pop the trunk. "Hey buddy, I've got some old clothes here. They should be about your size. I didn't make it in time to get them to the Goodwill store. Take your pick of 'em."

Stepping back, he grumbled, "Mister, I ain't lookin' for no trouble." He wipes his nose on his sleeve before holding his hands up, hoping to ward me off.

"No, no, no. Don't worry. I have a ten-dollar bill here I can spare if you're hungry."

"Gotta say I missed my meal at the shelter today. So, yeah, I guess I wouldn't say no to a couple bucks."

"You bet. Come on over and take a look what I've got in the trunk. There's even a jacket that'll keep you warm and dry if this weather gets any worse. There's a storm coming."

The homeless man takes a hesitant step toward the car. As he does, I draw my double-edged switchblade knife and press the release slide. Hearing the mechanical, spring-loaded double click of the out-front blade, his eyes fly wide open, though too late for him to react. He lets out a dreadful cry as I take a step forward, reach out, making two deft swipes with the knife; the first, a powerful stroke from the right severs his trachea, and the second, a backhand from the left, opens his right carotid artery. Stunned, he falls to his knees, choking and gasping, unable to utter a sound. I step back to avoid the spray of blood from his neck and admire my handiwork as his remarkably meaningless life drains from him.

CHAPTER 7

TAMPA POLICE MAJOR Lionel Davidson entered the Paladin Detective Agency offices with the boisterous greeting. "Hello? Anyone home here?"

"How the hell are you, Leo. Hang up your wet stuff and grab a seat."

Leo, as his friends called him, was a big, broad-shouldered giant of a black man. At six foot seven inches, weighing 270 pounds, he was an intimidating figure. His eyes were more golden than brown and his close-cropped, receding hairline showed as a widow's peak. But that's not what you noticed about him. It was his wide mouth, framing a tooth-filled smile that first caught your eye.

Kyle recalled how they first became friends, working together as young detectives at the Chicago Police Department more than twenty years earlier. Davidson, always the company man, took a promotion first to lieutenant, then to captain grade, which he held a number of years before retiring to Florida and settling in the Tampa area. With his stellar CPD credentials, he applied for, and earned, a major's position with the Tampa Police Department.

While hanging his dripping rain gear on the coat rack, Leo said, "Jesus, Kyle, I almost lost my hat twice walking from the car to your door. The chief's just put the entire department on emergency standby until Marcos passes."

Kyle rose to shake Leo's hand. "I heard that Marcos may bypass us."

"Yeah, but the chief's taking no chances. Current NOAA forecasts have downgraded it to Cat 2. It's turning east, and heading south of Orlando. I hope they're right, because if it was to hit this city head-on, the storm surge alone would knock us offline for a week. The Hillsborough River'd be halfway up your stairs here. Keep your fingers crossed. I'm told there hasn't been a storm like that here in almost a hundred years."

"Do you remember the snowstorm in Chicago back in '67? Fifty mile-an-hour winds, and a blizzard that dropped over two feet in one day. It took us three days to dig out of that one. Snowdrifts up to the eaves. Still a record."

"Boy do I. Didn't have a snow blower. Had to dig out with shovels," with a swipe at his brow.

"Mykel and I haven't seen you or Camille for what, a month now? Don't tell me policing is keeping you too busy for your friends these days."

"Nah. Well, maybe. Some days. One day you can't get your butt off your seat and out of the office and the next one, all hell breaks loose. It's the same in my office as it is for you," he said, gesturing toward 7th Avenue, "but I've got fifty more employees than you.

"But never mind that. How's Mykel doing these days? Poor woman. She's got the temperament of a saint to tolerate your crusty-ass disposition. And you're wrong. It's been well over a month now since we've gotten together."

"Oh, c'mon. Has it really? Funny, Mykel never complains about my manners. She's still busy working at Tampa General, but we manage to get out on weekends on the *Floribbean Flow*.

"So, how's Camille? You have to join us again one weekend soon. How about a picnic on Caladesi Island?"

"Sure, we'd love to hit the high seas with you two again. Camille's good, thanks.

"Thank God Marcos is veering east. Tell me you and Mykel haven't canceled your wedding plans."

"No, we're still on for the thirteenth. Let's have the ladies to work decide on an day out together after the wedding."

"Great." And then, searching Kyle's eyes for a second, he sighed before saying, "Wish I could say the same about things downtown. One of the reasons I came by this morning is because I could use some of your expertise on a case. It's one that's putting enormous pressure on the department. There's a serial killer who's just taken down his third homeless vic in Ybor. His M.O. is two slashes to the throat."

"I haven't read anything about it in the papers. Have you been keeping them out of it?"

"No, not directly. They've cooperated with us 'til now. But, with this third vic, they're going to release the story. And, our perp has taken a fancy to poetry and started dropping twisted verses at the Trib's office. Calls himself 'Y2K.'"

"I'm sure you already have a team working it, so why are we talking about this Leo?"

"I've got a team, but they haven't delivered diddly yet. The storm from the chief has begun to pour down on me."

"Yeah, I've felt it myself. You remember that doofus, Commander Rouse, at the Chicago PD, I'm sure. He's one of the main reasons I left the department and moved here to go private."

"I sure do. I was sorry for you after I left and moved over to Area Three. He was always a classless act. His personality struck me like a cockroach on a birthday cake.

"So here's what I'm hoping you'll do for me, Kyle. Would you take a look at this guy's poetry and share your ideas of what's going on in this perp's head? That's one of your strengths, and I could use some of that now."

"Absolutely. I'd be happy to give you my thoughts. Do you have it with you?"

Pulling a piece of paper from his uniform pocket, Leo handed it to Kyle.

Kyle read the lines:

> *Second Horseman's Here!*
> *World That Was Now Crashes Down.*
> *Your People IT's Failed...*
> *- Don't Guess Who I Am, Just Ask*
> —Y2K.

"First thing, I recognize this style of verse. This guy's no poet laureate, but it follows one of the traditional forms of a Japanese Haiku. The first line has five syllables, the second seven, and the third also has five.

"Next, in the third line, the word 'IT' is capitalized. That's important. Read one way, 'Your people *it's* failed.' However, I'd guess the capitalization of that word is deliberate, altering its sense to imply that IT, an acronym for Information Technology, has failed the people and ties in with his signature, 'Y2K.'

"His reference to the second horseman no doubt points to the apocalyptic section of the Bible's Revelations. That's the one riding a red horse, and is the harbinger of war who stirs man's inhumanity to man. The last line, *'Don't Guess Who I Am, Just Ask–Y2K,'* has to be a clue to his identity. It's a tease. And, there's something about the juxtaposition of 'Don't Guess,' and 'Just Ask,' that interests me. I'll need to give that some more thought.

"Finally, the signature, 'Y2K,' may be a reference to what's being touted on the internet these days as the possible collapse of the world's internet and financial systems. Analysts worry it will occur when the calendar changes over from December 31st, 1999 to January 1st, 2000. There's big time concern in many business and government IT shops.

They fear it could corrupt date calculations and create serious problems with their software."

"How's that?" Leo asked.

"It has to do with the idea that since the early days of computer programming, in order to keep their program's memory use economical, they only formatted dates in a three-part series of two-digits. So, today's date in their programs read one-one, zero-two, ninety-nine, using only two digits each for month, day, and year. The concern is when January first, two-thousand arrives, their programs will mis-read the year '00' as nineteen hundred rather than two thousand. That would be pretty dramatic since our pay dates, banking transactions, actuarial tables, and birth dates would all be off by a hundred years. You talk about chaos; that's chaos times one hundred."

"*Damn!*" Leo said.

"This nut case imagines he's the legendary red rider written of in Revelations. He wants to stir up fear and bloodshed in the world, while riding with a great sword on some fantastical horse. Talk about delusional…

"Has he left any evidence at the scenes? footprints, finger-prints, or DNA?"

Leo shook his head. "*Nada.* We believe he drives to the locations, engages his targets long enough to draw them close, then strikes. Quick in and quick out. No tire tracks or footprints yet. So far, they're all homeless men. From what the M.E. tells me, he uses a razor-sharp double-edged knife to slash their throats. Lots of blood at the scenes, but it's all from the vics."

"Double-edged? How does the M.E. know that?

"Fresh cuts on each side of the throat slashes; both clean.

"And homeless men, you say? He must be carrying a boatload of bad baggage concerning the dispossessed. I'd love to hear what the shrinks have to say. I've read most serial actors choose vics they don't believe will be missed, and this killer's choices support that premise."

"Kyle, this has been a huge help to me. I'll share your ideas with my Y2K team. I'll also get the department's shrink working on the motivation angle…but, would it be an imposition if I asked you to consult with my team on this case?"

"Now wait a second Leo. That's a mile past asking for an opinion."

Leo leaned forward in his seat. "Don't turn me down right away Kyle. I've given this some consideration. I'd make arrangements with our payroll department to bring you in as a consultant. We'll pay you at your hourly rate plus twenty-five percent. Why don't you meet my team so we can share some of your thoughts with them."

"Leo, sorry, but I'm not sure I could give this any quality attention. Business at Paladin Detective Agency is growing. I'm up to my elbows in alligators right now. Enough so, I'm looking to bring in a partner. I'm planning to ask my former partner in Chicago, Tony Petrocelli, about relocating to join me here. He's a young kid, but he's clever as a fox and has great instincts for this work."

"I know this offer comes from out of the blue, but this has been on my mind since we found the second victim. You tracked and caught the serial slaughterer, Slugger, several years back in Chicago, and my guess is, you'd be a boon to us on this Y2K case. While I confirm the arrangements with the department, please, take a day or two to consider my offer, okay?"

"I'll consider it my friend. No promises."

"Fair enough."

Kyle drew a notepad from his pocket and grabbed a pen. "On another note, could I ask a favor of you? I've just been employed by a new client, a Jolene Papadapolis. She was involved in an auto accident on the 25th of last month. Could you check your department's records and see if the investigating officers gave it proper attention and follow-up? She claims she was run off the road and driven into a tree.

"The officers reported being suspicious of her behavior, and they administered a breathalyzer. She blew .07 on it. In Florida, .08 gets you an automatic trip to lockup and a DUI conviction. But she claims they never bothered to investigate the scene. She's got other problems that may be related, but I told her I'd follow-up."

"No problem. Give me her name and the date. I'll let you know if I find any issues with their procedures."

CHAPTER 8

NOVEMBER 2, 1999, 11:00 A.M.
(THREE DAYS EARLIER)

MARCOS HAD TURNED northeast. The winds were still fierce and the rain relentless, but local emergency alerts had fallen. Orlando and Daytona were now Marcos's targets.

Kyle stopped for lunch at the Sagua La Grande Cantina. Guillermo greeted him in his usual energetic fashion from behind the counter, "Hola amigo!" Without waiting for a response, he added, "Hungry today? I am serving a favorite sandwich of mine, the *Media Noche,* the Cuban Midnight. I make this with a sweet Cuban bread and my very special *picante* sauce," he said, his lips pursed while his right-hand gestured spreading fingers from his mouth." And I serve with fried plantains and a Frutabomba milkshake."

After sitting in the Guadalupe Room, Kyle said, "Count me in for the Cuban and plantains, but what on earth is a Frutabomba milkshake?"

"It is what you call papaya. I use it because the native fruit I used in Cuba, the Mamey, is not easy to get in Florida. I guarantee you love it."

Kyle lifted the menu to hide his smile. "And if I don't?"

Guillermo bowed slightly with arms crossed and right hand over his heart. "If you do not, I do not charge you,"

"In that case, bring it on."

After finishing his meal, Kyle hailed the owner. "I'll be paying for my lunch. The sandwich and shake were as good as you promised. Your shake reminds me of the strawberry malts I loved as a boy in Ireland. It's not too sweet, but has a rich, cantaloupe-like flavor. Your recommendations never disappoint."

"You are very kind." Guillermo leaned in closer and lowered his voice. "But, may I beg a favor from you, to stay for a moment?"

"Of course. Please sit."

When Guillermo joined Kyle, Rosa breezed over to ask, "Would either of you like a Cuban coffee or espresso?"

Guillermo shook his head and sat down.

"Thank you, but I've had enough. By the way, with Hurricane Marcos's passing, the weather for the wedding will be perfect."

"Wonderful news! I am so excited for you and Mykel," she said.

As Rosa walked away, Guillermo inhaled deeply, and said, "I wish to tell you of my friend. He was killed last night."

Surprised, Kyle said, "Who is it? What happened?"

"He was a man who lived here in Ybor. He was a good man, but one with no home. He stay under a bridge at the highway. A kind man, always respectful; a veteran. He come to my back door to ask for food; never bossy or angry like some who come. His true name was Armando, but people call him *Queasy*. He says he got the, ah, *como se dice, name-of-the-nick?* when he cook for the army."

"You mean nickname?"

"Sí, nickname. He says that is how he make all his meals, quick and easy."

Kyle interrupted, "Hold on a moment. I spoke with Leo today. He asked if I could help with these recent murders in the parks. This may be the same man. If I'm able to, I will. Tell me, have you heard about any other murders in the parks here in Ybor recently?"

"It is not in the paper, but there are two before. Men tell me that the parks, at night, are more safe than shelters. But now, they are afraid. I will ask my friends. They will tell me if they hear more."

"That will help. I'll pass along anything you hear to Leo."

"Now I feel bad, but this is what I need to ask of you. Will you try to find this man who kills my friend? It is not right to ask this, but I will pay you. I am very fond of Mr. Queasy, and I would love to put his soul at peace by having you catch this terrible person that takes his life."

"I understand, *mi asere*. I'm the only person at my agency right now. But, please give me a day or two to figure out if there's some way I can help you."

CHAPTER 9

NOVEMBER 2, 1999, 1:45 P.M.
(THREE DAYS EARLIER)

KYLE SAT AT his desk combing through his note-scribbled planner. He puzzled over how to cooperate with TPD on the Y2K case and find Queasy's murderer for Guillermo. The way it seemed now, there was no way in hell he'd do it without help. Time to call Tony?

This wasn't the first time he'd considered it. In the last six months, the agency grew fast, and cases were piling up higher than logs on a bonfire. The past two weeks alone, he'd contracted for a missing persons case, an insurance fraud claim involving corporate larceny, and a cold case inquiry. And now a new client, Jolene Papadapolis, who claims she's being threatened by strangers, was on her way to talk with him.

The need for decisive action stirred him from his torpor. Time to make the call.

JOLENE PAPADAPOLIS BURST into the office at 2:10. Wearing sunglasses, she was panting and her face was flushed. Her rain jacket was blown open and her umbrella turned outside in.

Kyle stood to greet her. "Hello…Ms. Papadapolis? What happened to you?"

"Damn hurricane practically blew my clothes off, but never mind that; there's a man in front of your building. He tipped his hat to me; damn suspicious looking fella if you ask me. He scared me, so I dashed up the stairs."

"Please, let me hang up your coat and umbrella for you. I'm glad you made it, in spite of this stormy weather. Please, have a seat. Can I get you a cup of coffee or a glass of water?"

"Well, since it's probably too early for a Piña Colada, coffee'd be fine, I guess." She squinted and blinked as she removed her sunglasses.

Kyle brought her coffee and went to the windows overlooking 7th Avenue. Wanting to reassure Jolene and give her a moment more to compose herself, he said, "Give me a moment to check downstairs." Donning a hooded poncho, Kyle went down and stepped onto the sidewalk. A near gale-forced wind whistled through the grating of the iron corbels supporting the balcony. The gusting rain out of the north-east had Kyle's rain poncho stuck to his body. He looked like he was vacuum-wrapped in yellow cellophane. Hooding his eyes with his hands, he scanned left and right. No sign of other people nearby.

He returned to the office and shook off his wrap. "Sorry Jo, I saw no suspicious men outside. Is it possible it might have been an innocent gesture from a polite passer-by? Or even someone just trying to keep their cap on their head? That wind's pretty wicked out there."

"Well, maybe. Now I'm settled a bit, I guess he didn't really seem *all that* dangerous. Kinda nerdy. Not like those bastards stalking me."

"Yes, you mentioned that you're being stalked, Ms. Papadapolis."

"Yeah. But hey, we agreed you'd be calling me Jo."

"Of course, Jo. But first, I'd like to hear more about your car accident."

Kyle opened his Papadapolis case folder. "I spoke to my friend at the police department and he'll review the accident report. He'll also speak with the officers involved. If he finds any problems, I'll let you know."

Looking directly into his eyes, Joanne smiled and said, "Thank you. Those cops treated me poorly. They assumed I was drunk from the get-go. That was flat out wrong. I swear to you. Like I told you, I was forced off the road."

"I understand. And, I plan to visit the crash site to see if there might be something the officers missed that night. I'll report to you after.

"Now, about your suspicions that people are stalking you. Have you been directly threatened by anyone?"

"Well, no. Not directly."

"How about the people you regularly come into contact with; friends, neighbors, members of your church, or other groups you may belong to."

"My neighbors envy my beautiful home, but they say nothing more than 'Who's your landscaper?' or 'Where'd you buy your drapes?' They're shallow as mud puddles.

"We regularly go to church at the Sacred Heart. My husband, that's Dominic, props up their fundraising activities. He handles all the money stuff. I'm stuck trying to coddle the wives who just *love* pretending to be holier-than-thou. They probably think I'm a little highfalutin, but I don't believe I've made any blood enemies there."

"No one? Maybe someone who might have felt stung or slighted by what you call your 'highfalutin' attitude?"

She gave her head a slow shake and said, "Nah, I'm sure. Dom would've told me. Honestly, the only reason he takes me with him is to show me off, like some kind of rhinestone bauble. I'm a God-fearing woman Kyle, but if I had my druthers, I'd just as soon stay home and drink Margaritas. I grew up in a Baptist community, and that suited me just fine."

Jolene hesitated momentarily, tugged at the hem of her skirt and coughed into her hand. She straightened, waiting for Kyle to ask another question.

She blushed and coughed again before continuing. "Yes, well I do get together with my astrology group every week. I've been studying for years. There's a group of us who meet to talk about chart making, zodiac signs, planetary influences, and the like.

"Actually, it's my latest charts that started me worrying. My daily charts are highlighting a dire conjunction of Mercury and the moon in Pisces."

"I see. Any problems with any of the women in your group?"

"Well, one member, Gabby Rostock, has been a pain in my ass lately. She's been fussin' at me a lot. She argues with me about my use of spiritual influences and my chart interpretations. I'm sure she's the one whispering to the others that I'm clueless."

"Is it possible her 'fussiness' could be more than simple rivalry?"

"I wouldn't have thought so a month ago. But her blood has risen lately. We don't talk after meetings like we used to."

"If it's okay with you, I'd like to speak with her. Please provide me with her contact information."

"Sure."

"Good. Anything else you recall that could help me?"

"No, not right now, but if I think of anything, I'll let you know."

"With your permission, I'd also like to speak with your husband. He may be able to provide me with further information. How would you describe your relationship, Jo?"

Jolene blanched, and momentarily gazed beyond the windows. Then, turning back to Kyle, she said, "I'd like to say we have one of those Hollywood marriages you read about in the papers. But truth be told, our relationship has swirled into the toilet lately. Most of our conversations involve how he's disappointed in me."

Kyle sat back. "Why? Do you suspect he doesn't believe you?"

"No...well maybe." Then sighing, "There's been telltales. When I talk with him about my fears, he poo-poos them."

"How do you mean?"

"He scoffs and tells me I'm imagining it."

"Why do you think he says you 'disappoint' him, Jo?"

Jolene shifted in her seat and averted her eyes. "He tells me I drink too much. Also says I'm not as attentive to him as I used to be. I mean, that happens in most marriages, right? And, he calls me paranoid. He doesn't like it when I fuss about stuff." *Like my recent chronic headaches.*

"I understand, Jo. But I'd like to speak with him. Would that be okay?"

"If it'll help you, then yeah, sure. But you gotta' promise not to tell him we spoke about our marriage. It'd only make my troubles with him worse."

"I'll respect that. My only purpose will be to find out how your life may be in jeopardy." Then, with a confident smile, "And Jo, I'm good at what I do."

"Thank you so much, Kyle! But I need a favor from you. You have to let me chart your horoscope, okay? To do that, I'll need your birth information. Without it, I won't be sure of the best way to work with *you*." Then, with a crooked smile and an exaggerated wink, she added, "That's also the least I can do for the man who holds my life in his hands."

CHAPTER 10

TWO HOURS LATER, Kyle called Tony Petrocelli. "Hello Tony! How are ya?"

"Hey Kyle. Glad you called. I'm doing okay here up in the cold white north. It's 22 degrees today and my windows are rattling. Jeeeezus! How'd you and Mykel make out with that hurricane? On the news, they said it was gonna' be bad."

"Lots of wind and rain, but the worst of it flew by us to the east. Marcos decided it would rather blow down houses in Orlando than Tampa. 22 degrees? Damn, I'm reminded why I moved south.

"So glad it blew by you."

"Ready for my wedding day on the thirteenth? Mykel and I are both excited to see you again, best man."

"Don't worry Kyle, I'll get you to the church on time."

"Remember, I told you, no bachelor party with endless shots of Irish Whiskey and Cream with a Guinness. None of that tomfoolery for me, thank you."

"Tomfoolery? That sounds like one of my words. But you're breakin' my heart." Kyle pictured Tony's comical frown. "But hey, let's save that discussion for when I've got Patrick beside me…"

"There'll be time enough for celebrating at the reception. Listen Tony, I just spoke with Leo Davidson this morning. He's now a major here at the Tampa PD. From description I gave of you, he believes you're some sort of wunderkind."

"Thanks. That just might come in handy if I'm ever scouting work down your way."

"Now you mention it, tell me, how are things in Chicago these days?" he said, hoping for the right answer.

"Remember that saying Sam Weller endlessly spouted, 'S-O-S-D-D,' *Same Old Shit, Different Day*. I can't catch a break here between Commander Rouse's tirelessly useless grousing about 'the book,' and a rookie partner who's got no respect for the citizens we're ostensibly protecting.

"Got me thinking about changes I could make. I have my GI Bill, a modest stash of money in the bank, and I'm still young enough for a career change. I've been taking computer courses at the College of DuPage. Turns out, I have a knack for them. Who knew? Any advice?"

Yes! "You're right, Sam Weller was a character. My partner and best friend, right up until I discovered he was just a pathetic, immoral, murderer hiding behind a tired badge."

"It took us all by surprise."

"But hey Tony, I'm glad you asked my opinion. That's one of the reasons I called today. Things are going well for me here at the agency. I've got more work than I can handle and the money's better than I imagined it would be. I'm in a position where I need to hire a partner now. And Tony, honestly, you're the only person I'm considering.

Tony gulped.

"You mentioned a possible interest in working down this way. Ya know, we worked well together at CPD. You're a bright, creative detective with a scary amount of the same instincts I have. What would you say to an offer for work from me…right now?"

"Whaaaat! Kyle, are you serious? I mean, Holy shit! I'm blown away that you'd consider me. Holy shit! Are you serious?"

"Yep. I've been thinking about this for a couple months. You need to know, I wouldn't ask for an up-front buy-in from you. We'd spread it out over a few years. And, I'd agree to any arrangements you need to continue your computer coursework."

"Whaaaat! Goddamn! This is like a dream come true. If I say yes, how soon would you want me there? There'd be a good bit of stuff to finish here, and more to get settled down there. What'd be *your* timeline?"

"Tony, I'd be happy if you told me you'd be here tomorrow. Like I said, my work load here is exploding. I'm looking at an offer to consult with the Tampa PD on a serial killer case down here. Leo Davidson, my friend as a rookie in Chicago, is now a major here. He asked if I'd consider working on it. The money'd be good. But I can't do it without more hands-on-deck.

"I know it'll take time to close out your business at CPD and plan your moving arrangements, Tony. I'll give you an incentive, a relocation stipend to assist with the details. And there'd be no need to find a place here right away; Mykel and I'll be happy to put you up 'til you find a place."

"Man, Kyle, I'm really dumbfounded by your offer. Could you give me 24 hours to consider it? I need to speak with my folks; you know my family, they like me nearby—the whole Sunday night dinner thing, right?"

"Absolutely! Take your time. You need to know, if you decide not to do it, it won't affect our friendship. I'll respect your decision either way. Please, I insist, talk to your folks about it."

"I promise I will. And, with a mounting pitch in his voice, he said, *"Holy Shit!* I'm gonna need a bigger hat size now."

"Well, don't buy any new hats just yet. Trust me, I'll be working you like a plantation plow horse. Call me when you've settled on a decision Tony. We'll talk more then."

"I won't, I mean I will. I'll do…I'll do that."

CHAPTER 11

"HELLO, LEO. I'VE been considering your invitation. I'd like a chance to meet your Y2K team. I don't want to step into an ongoing investigation if there's any pushback from them; especially since I'd be an outside consultant."

"I agree Kyle. I've scheduled a meeting with them this morning at eleven. It'd be a good chance for you to meet them and learn where they are with the case. Join us then, okay?"

"I'll make the time, Leo. Why don't I come in early so we talk about the ground rules before I meet the team?"

"Sure. Be at my office at 10:30."

CHAPTER 12

RAISING HIS HEAD from a financial report he was reviewing, Dominic Papadapolis reluctantly answered his office phone. "Hello."

"Hello Mr. Papadapolis. This is Kyle McNally with the Paladin Detective Agency. I'm sure you're aware, your wife has hired me to investigate possible threats to her life. She suggested you two have discussed this, right?"

Papadapolis sighed. "Yes, yes, we have. But frankly, I'm less than pleased about it, Mr. McNally. Her trouble started about a month ago with a horoscope prediction advising her to 'beware of strangers.' Then, after claiming she was driven off the road last week, she became more adamant. When I spoke with the police, they told me she was lucky she wasn't cited with a D.U.I.

"Honestly Mr. McNally, she's always been a little flakey. Don't get me wrong, I love her dearly, but every once in a while she has these spells that remind me that you can remove the girl from the trailer park, but you can't remove the trash from the girl."

Kyle's eyes widened. "I see. The reason for my call today, Mr. Papadapolis, is to arrange for a meeting to discuss any pertinent information that you may have. It will help me choose how to proceed. Any chance we could meet tomorrow morning? I'll come to your office if that's convenient."

"Mr. McNally, I'm preparing for an important overseas business trip in a couple of days. However, if you honestly believe I might be able to help, well then yes, I'll meet with you. I'll have my secretary schedule a meeting for us."

"Thank you, sir."

Kyle scratched a couple of hasty notes regarding questions he had for Mr. Papadapolis.

CHAPTER 13

NOVEMBER 3, 1999, 10:30 A.M.
(TWO DAYS EARLIER)

LEO DAVIDSON WELCOMED Kyle into his office. On entering, Kyle recoiled at the odor of hours-old, burnt coffee and shook his head when Leo gestured for him to grab a cup.

Covering the phone's mic, Leo said, "I'm glad you're here Kyle. Please sit. I need a moment."

While Leo spoke with the caller, Kyle scanned the office. There was a bookcase against one wall with procedure manuals, law books, binders, certificates, and award plaques. Leo sat behind a leather-topped oak wood desk stacked with bundled papers and manila folders. Behind Davidson stood a credenza with a variety of both official and personal photos. The third wall had a console table beneath a row of windows, displaying a panoramic view of downtown Tampa.

Davidson's office brought back unpleasant memories of that numbskull, Commander Rouse, from his last position with the Chicago PD—Kyle had seriously debated tossing Rouse out of his office window more than once.

He slipped into a chair just as Leo dropped the receiver back on its cradle. Noticing the man's reaction to the call, he said, "Rough day?"

Leo scoffed. "Understatement of the week. That was the chief, calling to remind me our crime stats haven't declined as much as he promised when appointed by the mayor. And now he expects us to perform that magic trick, even after the latest budget cuts; the ones he proposed."

"I get it Leo. Shit rolls downhill."

"Yeah, but I'll save that rant for another day. That's not why you're here."

"Sure. Let's pin down your expectations about my *possible* participation with your Y2K team. Can I expect the full cooperation of them? I'd want loose reins from you, Leo. You remember how I work. Also, I don't want to be bogged down with procedural bullshit and never-ending piles of written reports."

Leo shrugged. "And that'd get a big 'fuck you' from the chief. Much as I'd like to Kyle, I won't promise you *complete* autonomy. This is a police investigation, so you'll be answering directly to me. I'll call the shots about protocol. But if you run into any, and I mean *any*, trouble with either Lieutenant Willcox or his team members, Sergeant Dallas, or Corporal O'Shea, bring it to me. I know you, and I know these cops. I'll be able to handle their concerns.

"In Chicago, you were always the lead dog on your cases. It won't be quite like that here. But I will demand their cooperation. Anything else?"

"No. Thanks Leo, I'll be okay with that, for now. It looks like Tony Petrocelli will be joining me at Paladin. That'll open up my schedule, so I can join you and your team."

Both men stood and shook hands. "Congratulations Kyle. Anything else?

"No."

"Then let's go meet the team."

MAJOR DAVIDSON AND Kyle entered the windowless conference room and sat. The atmosphere crackled with tension.

"Kyle McNally, I'd like you to meet my Y2K team. The lead on this case is Lieutenant Nick Willcox. His team members include Detective Sergeant Ed Dallas, and Corporal Shannon O'Shea.

"Folks, Mr. McNally is here to meet you. Although he's told me that his firm, Paladin Detective Agency, is too busy to join us immediately, there's a chance that may change soon. In that case, he'd be working with us on the Y2K case.

"That's why Kyle is here today. This is what I'll expect if and when he should join us. First, your cooperation is non-negotiable. You will share all information with each other, whether it's interviews, reports, or evidential discovery. Second, stay in contact with each other. Any lack of communication may mean the difference between catching this heartless perp or him getting away. Finally, I am the be-all and end-all arbiter of any issues. Bottom line, I'll insist you work together as a team. Any questions?"

Glancing sideways at Dallas and O'Shea, Lt. Willcox rocked back in his chair, locked his hands behind his head and said, "I have a couple, major. Please remind me just exactly why we need a private dick consulting on this case. And, why McNally's qualified to join us," he said, with an exaggerated, pinched face.

"Glad you asked Nick. To your first question, after three murders by Y2K, this department has brought in and interrogated five suspects, but still no arrests. I appreciate your work so far, but...sorry Nick, we still don't have him. TPD and I are depending on you and your team to find and capture the son-of-a-bitch.

"As to your second question dealing with Kyle McNally's credentials, he's a retired former Chicago police detective with over twenty years of service. He led the investigation several years back that snagged the maniacal serial killer, the 'Slugger,' one of the most notorious murderers in recent history. That guy committed at least seven slayings, both intrastate and interstate, when Kyle and his team tracked and captured him. And that's only one from a lengthy list of his bona fides.

"I'm sure you don't like being questioned about your techniques or results, Nick. Nobody does. But the pressure on my department is rising. This night stalker will soon be known to the community because the Tribune is going to press with his malevolent, cryptic poetry. Kyle has already given me several valuable insights into the mind of this deviant, and God knows we need that kind of help."

Red faced, Willcox leaned in and shot back, "Just so I'm reading you correctly, major, you expect us to treat this private dick like he's one of our own?" he said, spitting the question beneath narrowed eyes and a clenched jaw.

"Nick, this isn't a violation of protocol, *or* a challenge to your personal pride. Trust me, Kyle would be an asset to your team. I'm asking you to set aside your ego on this one. We need to do what's right for the department and the people of Tampa we're sworn to protect.

"Let me say again, should Kyle join us, I'm expecting your full cooperation with him." Then, while surveying the team, he ended with, "Is *that* clear people?"

Kyle jumped in, "If I may, major. Lieutenant Willcox, my role in your investigation would only be to provide you with whatever insights I have concerning the mind of Y2K. I'm told I'm good at that. After talking with Major Davidson, I may have an inkling of what this creep is thinking. He believes Armageddon is coming, and he wants to hasten the journey for those poor homeless men he's picked to be first in line. For whatever sick reason, he believes they need a personal escort to the other side.

"I'll share my ideas and discoveries with you and your team, and assist with any other aspects of this case I'm able to. Provided, however, that you honor your end of the arrangement and keep me informed of your findings. This is *your* case. That'll never be questioned. I hope I can help you catch this guy before any more itinerant citizens turn up dead on the streets of Ybor City."

Kyle sat back and offered a crisp nod to Leo.

"So, if there are no further questions," Major Davidson said, "let me get back to you later today on the status of the investigation going forward. Kyle and I will continue to discuss his decision. Thank you. That will be all."

"WELL KYLE, NOW that you've met the team, what do you think?"

"That Willcox would be happy if he found me run over by a truck on Dale Mabry Highway."

"Yeah, Nick can be a hard ass, but he's a good cop. This case's been tough on him. So, you figure you can work with them?"

Shaking his head, Kyle said, "If it were for the money alone, Leo, I'd say no. Willcox will probably try to hold his cooperation hostage. But Guillermo, at the Sagua La Grande, also asked for my help. Turns out, he knew this latest victim and was fond of him. He hopes I can help catch this miscreant.

"I'm waiting for Tony to call me back. If he says yes, then I'll make this happen. If not, sorry, but it'd just be too much for me. I didn't get into this business to disappoint my clients."

CHAPTER 14

IF MCNALLY HAD gotten over two hours of sleep last night, the jangling of his office phone wouldn't sound like a fire alarm. He was out most of the night on a skip trace. Grimacing, he pushed his coffee aside and reached for the phone.

"Paladin Detective Agency, Kyle McNally speaking."

"Hello Kyle. It's Tony."

"Hey Tony, I'm glad you called. What's up?"

"Does that offer you made me still stand?"

"Uh, offer? What offer?"

"Yeah, yeah, I get it. You're kidding, right?"

"Sorry, but I've been up all night on a skip trace. Please refresh my memory, Tony."

"Huh?"

Then smiling, "Of course I'm kidding. Did you make a decision? Will you be joining me at the agency?

"I'm gonna say yes!"

"That's terrific Tony. How about your family? Your parents okay with this?"

"Yes. I spoke with my parents. They're fully on board. My father said it is just the right offer at just the right time; even called it *destino,* that's destiny in Italian."

"How soon would you be able to move down here? From my end, sooner's better."

"I have more than a month's vacation time coming, so if I submit my separation papers tomorrow, it's possible for me to head your way by the middle of next week."

Kyle leaned back in his chair and sighed. "That'd be great. I'll tell Mykel; she was hoping you'd say yes. Of course, you'll be staying with us until you find a place of your own. Let me know if you need anything else from me, okay?"

CHAPTER 15

NOVEMBER 4, 1999, 10:00 A.M.
(ONE DAY EARLIER)

KYLE ENTERED THE offices of Black Dragon Security Solutions, on the thirtieth floor of the downtown Sykes Building, locally called, the 'Beer Can' building. In its spacious reception area, the rear wall décor included a floor-to-ceiling brick facade that backed a babbling waterfall with a narrow pond, complete with koi fish. Manicured palm trees framed the pond. Spotlights illuminated a huge, red stone slab etched with their company logo, an ornate black dragon, with the company's title beneath. The office was impressive, intimidating.

In researching the business, he learned they became an industry leader by selling computerized security applications to large international corporations with recognizable names and stock ticker symbols.

The receptionist glanced up and flashed a warm and inviting smile at the tall, attractive man with a chiseled jawline, jade green eyes, and impeccably groomed jet-black hair. She said, "Good morning, sir. How may I help you?"

"Hello. Kyle McNally, and I'm here for an appointment with Mr. Papadapolis."

"Oh yes, Mr. McNally, he's expecting you. Please have a seat. I'll notify him you're here."

While waiting, two men came out of Papadapolis' office talking together. One, who Kyle noted was unusually attired and clearly agitated, was slapping a fist onto the palm of his hand. On noticing him, they stopped speaking and quietly left the reception area.

Mr. Papadapolis stepped out of his office to greet Kyle. "Hello, Mr. McNally. Please come in and have a seat." Papadapolis wasn't much taller than the five-foot potted palm inside the room. He had a prominent chin, poorly disguised by a full, well-trimmed beard, topped by intense hooded eyes, and a clever smile.

"I hope I'm not interrupting a meeting."

"No, not at all. Those were two of my administrators. There was a disagreement and I was forced to clear the air." He chuckled and said, "They needed reminding that I will not keep lighting myself on fire just to keep them warm. It's not uncommon in corporate politics, and amplified in the services sector."

"Pressure rides in the driver's seat of the bus."

"That's the truth, and you can call me Dom. Please, sit. Would you like a cup of coffee, or something with a little more hair on it, Mr. McNally?"

"Thank you no, Dom. I'm good. Call me Kyle."

While Dom poured himself a fresh cup of coffee, Kyle surveyed the CEO's office. There was a collection of oversized artist-signed photographs depicting icy river scenes, flanked by snow-capped mountains in the background. All had an old-world artistic style, but shot with a contemporary eye. It was furnished with Danish modern pieces, reflecting spare architectural design and skinny, spikey steel legs. Kyle never liked the style.

There was a stand-up desk in one corner facing a bank of floor-to-ceiling windows. On it sat an open laptop computer and beside it, a framed picture of his wife, Jolene, wearing a ruby red, broad-brimmed floppy hat pulled low over both sides of her head, framing her face attractively. Sitting, he shifted a couple times, trying vainly to get comfortable until finally giving up, and leaning forward, elbows on his knees.

"To all appearances, your business is quite successful Dom. I read you're in the software security business. What exactly is it Black Dragon does?"

"Our business develops, markets, installs, and supports several computer software products. Our security package, *Dragon Safe*, is our flagship product and earns, by far, the lion's share of our revenue. A former brigade officer of mine, Felix Hermann, is my co-owner and Chief Sales and Marketing Officer. As a Lieutenant Colonel in the military during the Desert Storm operation, I was his superior officer and he was one of my company commanders. Now he's my captain here.

"We adapted our software in-house with my lead programmer, Scott Kaine. He was an officer under Captain Hermann and drove for me while serving in the Army's First Cavalry Division, Black Dragon Brigade. He studied computer programming and completed his degree while serving. He has a remarkable talent for it. Obviously, our unit was the namesake for my company.

"So, Kyle, you're here this morning concerning your investigation for my wife, correct?"

"Yes. She believes there are stalkers, or assailants, who are following her. I gathered from our previous phone conversation that you don't agree. Why is that?"

"Without wanting to get into the numerous *odd* stories from Jo's past, or her quirky diversions, this is just one more in a series of disturbing claims she's been known to make. None of those events previously involved either the police or a private investigator."

"Could you give me an example."

"The first time occurred soon after we were married; she tried to convince me that the insurance agent was defrauding us by charging for wind, flood, and hurricane damage on our policy. I was overseas then, and it took me a half a dozen phone calls and several faxes before convincing her the charges were legitimate."

"It sounds like that may have been a while back. Is there a more recent example?

Papadapolis sighed, "Several months ago, Jo was convinced that one of her "astrology" group members was plotting against her. She even accused the woman of poisoning her snack cookies.

"I'm meeting with one of the members of her astrology study group tomorrow. Jolene thinks she's trying to undermine her position, and thinks there may be a bigger issue behind it."

"That must be the woman she believed tried to poison her. Turns out it was only an allergy to anise seed. She's always been a bit of a prima donna, Kyle. And now…and now," he paused, heat rising on his cheeks, "now she's convinced she's being threatened by stalkers. Need I go on?"

"No, thank you, Dom. How long have you and Mrs. Papadapolis been married?"

"Fifteen years. I was a captain when we married. I rose to the rank of Lieutenant Colonel ten years after, and retired following a tour of duty in Iraq."

"Thank you for your service, Dom. Any other concerns about your wife's behavior?"

"None I'm prepared to share with you."

"And you're not convinced she was run off the road last week?"

"No. Not after learning that she was near the legal limit for a DUI."

"I ask because I spoke with my friend, a major with TPD this morning. He reviewed the crash scene report and tells me the officers who responded may not have completed a thorough investigation."

"Do you believe her claim that she *was* forced from the road?"

"Not with certainty. But I'm going to keep pursuing it, and will visit the scene myself. Give me another day or two on that."

"What you're telling me puts a different light on it." He paused a moment and shrugged, "Jo—how best to say it—is a less-than-reliable source of information. And the past month or two she's been even more unsteady. I'm concerned about her."

"I understand, Dom. A couple of last questions, if I may. Is there anyone who might possibly pose an actual threat to your wife? Have you received any unusual phone calls at home? Maybe someone calling and hanging up, or suspicious people in your neighborhood?"

"No, though some of our friends are aware she's high-strung, there's none who wish her harm. And no, no strange activity in or around our home that I've witnessed."

Recalling his conversation with Jolene, Kyle asked, "Dom, has your wife ever accused you of not listening to her concerns?"

Dom's eyes grew wide. "Why? Did she say anything to you? Listen, over the past year or two, our marriage has suffered. Between my business commitments and community involvements, it's been easy to let my personal life slip. But, once my company gets past its Y2K issues, I intend to devote more time to Jo."

Unwilling to explain further, he said, "No, not directly,"

His questions answered, Kyle stood and shook hands with Papadapolis, "Thank you for your time, Dom. May I speak with you again if I need more help?"

"Of course, Kyle. I'll consider it a favor if you'd keep me in the loop. It'd break my heart if anything were to happen to her."

CHAPTER 16

NOVEMBER 4, 1999, 2:00 P.M.
(ONE DAY EARLIER)

"**H**ELLO LEO. KYLE here. I've talked with Tony Petrocelli and he's agreed to join me at Paladin Detective Agency."

"That's great. Does that mean you'll be consulting with my Y2K team?"

"Yes, it does. Once Tony's here and I've got him situated, I'd like to meet with your team again before joining them."

"Glad to hear it. But, why another meet? Anything I need to know about?"

"It's Willcox. His reaction at our first meeting was a mile from welcoming."

"Like I told you, you let me deal with Nick, okay? He'll be my problem, not yours."

"If you say so. It will also give me a chance to learn more about the Bishop Park killing. Guillermo knew the vic and asked for my help finding the man's killer."

"What information did he give you about the man's identity?"

"Here's what I've got so far."

Leo grabbed a pen and began taking notes.

When Kyle finished, he said, "Thanks Kyle, that's more than we got in the past three days on our end. Tell Guillermo we're doing all we can, but ID-ing and tracking itinerants in a city the size of Tampa is about as easy as boning a marlin with a butter knife."

"I hear you. I'll share more as I learn more."

KYLE WALKED INTO Sagua La Grande Cantina at the tail-end of the lunch hour rush. Rosalina greeted him with a smile and said, "Hello Kyle. Where would you like to sit today?"

"Thanks Rosa, in the Guadalupe Room. Please ask Guillermo to join me when he's got a minute. I'd like to speak to him about his friend Queasy,"

"Certainly. He'll be happy to hear that. May I bring you a Cuban coffee or an espresso?"

"Espresso and a glass of water would be great, thanks."

By the time Kyle's coffee was served, Guillermo was seated at the table.

"I'm glad you are here, *mi asere*. Rosa tell me you want to talk."

"Yes, Guillermo. I've got some good news for you. I talked with Tony Petrocelli, my former partner at the Chicago Police Department. He's agreed to move to Florida and join me at the agency."

"What good news! You say you hoped for him to come."

"With Tony here, I can take on additional cases."

"Will you be helping to find the killer of my friend, Queasy, then?"

"Yes, I will, though I'll need more information about Queasy. Have you got a moment to speak more about it?" Kyle took a notepad from his shirt pocket and continued. "I'll need any and all the information you have, Guillermo. I believe you said Armando is his given name, correct?"

"Sí."

"Did you know his last name?"

Guillermo cleared his throat and stroked his chin. "Not for sure, but he say, Alonso, or maybe Alfonso. I should pay closer attention."

"Don't worry, that's a start. Did he tell you where he was from? His home town or any other places he'd been to?"

"Sí. he say he come from Juárez, Mexico. When he was little, his parents move up north, to Ohio, I think."

"Any idea where he kept his belongings…or, where he slept?"

"Queasy say he didn't like a shelter. Too much stealing and fighting with people there. As a army veteran, he tell me he can take care of himself. He sleep under a bridge on 34th Street. I worry much for him. He was my friend. I hope this help you."

"It'll get me started. I promise, I'll do what I can to find the man who murdered your friend."

CHAPTER 17

NOVEMBER 4, 1999, 6:00 P.M.
(ONE DAY EARLIER)

KYLE EXHALED SLOWLY, releasing the weight of the week from his shoulders as Tomaso Albinoni's dulcet Violin Concertos played softly in the background. "This has been a hell of a week, my love. I've hired Tony Petrocelli, a bright young partner; took on an interesting new client, a wealthy astrologer who claims she's being stalked; and told Leo Davidson I'll be consulting with him on a serial killer case at TPD."

"I'd say so," Mykel responded. Then, with a tilt of her head and a sweet smile, "Does it also suggest the time may be right for you to find the receptionist you've been procrastinating about, Detective McNally?"

"You're right, but when did my first name become *detective*?" Then suggestively grinning, "though don't get me wrong—it's sexy as hell the way you say it."

They were relaxing comfortably at the dining room table, having just finished a steak dinner Kyle prepared. Mykel tossed a Caesar Salad with her scratch-made dressing. They'd almost finished an excellent bottle of Italian Valpolicella wine with the meal. The air in the room still held the heady aromas of smoked wood and island spice.

Mykel's smile was warm and inviting as she raised her glass in a toast, and said, "Congratulations, Detective, President and CEO of the Paladin Detective Agency. I'm divinely happy for you, my love. Your business is taking off, and things are looking up for me at Tampa General. Did I mention there's scuttlebutt I'm being considered for a promotion to Staff Director?"

"No, you didn't." Then raising his glass, "To my brilliant, lovely forensic doctor, and wife-to-be. May our lives be filled with countless days like today, darling."

Mykel sucked in a breath, winked, and replied, "I love it when you talk that way, *detective*. I'm so excited about our plans for tomorrow. I'm joining a few girls from the hospital for lunch at Cigar City Pizza. Can you pick me up after? We should be done by one. Then, you and I can head over to City Hall, pick up our marriage license, and take the rest of the afternoon off. How's that sound?" as the music reached a crescendo.

"And how about after, we hop on board the Floribbean Flow and cruise over to the Crab House on Tierra Verde for a sunset dinner; you love their steamed Blue Crab." He flashed her a playful smile and set his empty wineglass on the table. "But in the meantime…let's finish this conversation in the bedroom."

The allegro was just beginning. Mykel needed no further incentive. "I dare not ignore my private dick's request," she said with a nod and a playful nudge. "Meet me there in five, or suffer the consequences of conjugal rejection."

Kyle entered the bedroom, lit only by the full moon's glow, which danced around the room like shimmering fireflies. Admiring his seductive fiancée lying on their bed beckoning to him with her arms open wide, his breath caught in his throat. He knew he never loved or wanted a woman more.

They would cherish the promises, the passion, and the shared love, as omens of their long, happy lives together.

CHAPTER 18

NOVEMBER 4, 1999, 8:00 P.M.
(ONE DAY EARLIER)

DOMINIC PAPADAPOLIS, FEELING good as he stepped onto his patio, was whistling a snatch from Third Eye Blind's, *Losing A Whole Year,* playing on the car radio. He liked the sentiment.

The sun had set hours earlier. The intoxicating fragrance of late-blooming jasmine hung in the air like a scented lady's handkerchief.

He bent over his wife, Jolene, and kissed her on the forehead. Startled, her Old-Fashioned cocktail first splashed, then tipped, before slipping from her hand and shattering on the stone pavers.

"Jesus Christ, Dom! You scared the hell out of me." Her hands were shaking.

"Didn't mean to, darling. I thought you heard me coming."

With one hand over her mouth, she unsteadily staggered to her feet and said, "I'm sorry. B-but don't worry, no big deal. You, sit while I get this cleaned up.

"You like a cocktail? I think I'll fix myself a fresh one."

"Yeah, Jo, I could use one; been a tough day."

"Now sit. You look tired. It'll only take me a moment."

Ten minutes later, the two of them were seated with their drinks.

"I had a visit today from Kyle McNally."

She flinched. "I hope he didn't bother you too much. I asked him not to."

"Nah. He told me he's been in touch with the police department; said he'll be looking into your accident further. Anything I need to know about your meeting with him?"

Looking at their colorfully illuminated marble fountain, she said, "I hope this isn't going to cost you too much."

"Don't worry about that."

"He seems like a capable professional."

"I got that impression. Did you tell him about the stalkers?"

"A little. He's gonna focus on the accident first."

Dom began twirling the fruit around in his drink. "So, you think he believes you about being driven off the road?"

Looking back at the fountain, "I dunno. Maybe."

Dom downed his cocktail and stood. "I'm about done in. I think I'll head up to the bedroom."

Her forehead dipped down, but with her eyes squarely on him, she whispered, "You like some company? I'd be happy to help calm you." Then, with a sly grin, "You know how much I like doing that for you."

"That'd be nice."

CHAPTER 19

NOVEMBER 5, 1999, 12:45 P.M.
(THE PRESENT)

KYLE PARKED IN a lot across the street from the Cigar City Pizza Parlor, waiting to meet Mykel. When he caught sight of her, she waved to him. As he got out of his car, a man stepped behind her.

Without warning, her head jerk backward and arms flailed out as her face contorted from a smile into a horrified look of shock.

He recoiled in shock as a spray of blood burst from the front of her blouse. She and the man behind her collapsed to the pavement.

Stunned, Kyle froze for a moment. *No, that isn't Mykel*! His heart pounding wildly, he dashed across the street.

He knelt beside Mykel, checking her neck for a pulse. There was none. Kyle tore off his shirt, compressing the wound on her chest, hoping she might still have a chance. He lifted her into his arms, hugging her, while shouting, "Someone, *please* call 911!"

Oblivious to the growing chaos around him, he held her close. *Darling, please don't leave me. Mykel, open your eyes. Please don't go. Don't die. Don't leave me now. Please.*

He shouted again, "Someone call 911!"

Gently laying Mykel back on the pavement, Kyle stood, drew his sidearm, holding its muzzle up in the high-ready position. He searched the nearby crowd. Many were shouting and running in fear for their lives. Automobile horns became near deafening when one couple bolted into the street and were struck by a delivery truck.

Kyle moved to the second victim. He'd taken a bullet to the back of his skull; his face was obliterated. A single bullet killed them both; likely a high velocity shot fired from a sniper's rifle. There was no second shot.

The clamor of the panicked crowd reached a crescendo, but Kyle ignored it as he now focused his full attention on locating the gunman who'd murdered Mykel. He rotated gradually, searching every face, every back, every nearby doorway and window, seeking any sign of the shooter. No one stood out. He concluded the shot had come from above and behind the victims.

By the time he was aware of the police and emergency vehicle sirens, his mind was circling like a Ferris Wheel. *This couldn't be happening!* The love of his life, Mykel, lay on the pavement beside him in a pool of blood, dead.

CHAPTER 20

FIRST RESPONDERS ASSESSED the conditions of the two people shot and the couple struck by a vehicle in the street. Kyle knelt and placed his weapon down as the responding officers approached him, guns drawn. He raised his hands slowly; one holding his private investigator license and concealed carry permit.

"Identify yourself and explain why you're here carrying a weapon," the officer demanded, ignoring Kyle's ID.

Kyle moved slowly, handing the officer his identification. "My name is Kyle McNally, officer. I'm a licensed private investigator. I hold a concealed carry permit from the State of Florida. I came to meet my fiancée, Mykel Hartley, lying there," pointing at Mykel with a slow, sallow-faced shake of his head. He stood in shock as the medical attendants lifted Mykel onto a gurney.

The taller one asked, "Did you shoot them?" as his partner began taking notes.

Kyle's eyes reddened while his fists clenched at that question. "No. Like I said, I was here to meet her when she was shot. We were going to apply for a marriage license today. She and the other victim both fell there. I had my gun drawn on the chance a shooter might still be nearby."

"Do you recognize the second victim?"

"His face is gone. So no, I don't recognize him."

"You were eyewitness to the crime, Mr. McNally. Please describe what you saw."

"I'd parked across the street in that lot," he said, pointing, "when I first saw Mykel, my fiancée."

"To confirm, you say she's your fiancée? Last name Hartley? I'm sorry, sir."

"Yes, that's right. Just as she waved to me, she and the man standing behind her lurched forward, like someone shoved them from behind. By the time I reached them, she was already dead. It was obvious the man died instantly from the gunshot to his head. As a former Chicago police detective, I began searching the immediate vicinity for a shooter."

One of the first officers finished cordoning off the immediate area with crime scene tape.

A police SUV pulled over, siren chirping and lights flashing. Major Lionel Davidson stepped out from the driver's side, while a uniformed officer exited the passenger side. They approached the two policemen standing near Kyle, who had turned away from them. Major Davidson addressed the first one, "Hello Corporal Swayze. I heard the broadcast about a shooting here. Lt. Willcox and I were nearby and came immediately. Were you first on the scene?"

"Yes, major. Corporal Ramirez and I responded to the scene at 13:09 p.m. sir. Best we determine was it's a shooter fired at two pedestrians standing together on the sidewalk. No other victims from gun fire. There was another couple injured when they ran in front of a truck attempting to flee the scene. No status on their condition yet. The truck driver is standing over there, sir."

"Good work Swayze. The M.E. is on the way. Lieutenant Willcox will take over from here. Has the crime scene team been contacted yet?"

"Yes sir. They're on their way."

Glancing over, Leo caught sight of the shirtless Kyle. "Kyle?" He walked over, extending a hand in greeting. "What are you doing here?" Then, noticing Kyle's pallor, asked, "What the hell's happened?"

"Leo, Mykel's dead."

"My God! Mykel? How on earth did that happen? Did you witness it?"

"Yes. One moment she's standing there waving at me and the next she's collapsed on the sidewalk, dead." Kyle lowered his head and turned away. When he'd recovered his composure, he continued, "Leo, what'll I do?" Looking directly into the eyes of his friend, he groaned, "What'll I do? I never saw my life without her."

Leo wrapped his arms around his friend to console him. "Kyle, we'll spare no resources to find the killer and make sure he's caught and brought to justice. I'm here with you, my friend. I promise to stand by you." Then whispering in his ear, "and trust me, today will be this asshole's last good day on earth."

Leo called to Corporal Ramirez, "Officer, get this man a shirt."

Teeth clenched, Kyle glared at his friend through swollen, bloodshot eyes. "Don't worry, Leo. *I'll* get this guy. I swear I'll burn his world down."

Leo was quick to respond. "Please, Kyle, go, take care of Mykel now. We need to get the second victim ID'd and take care of those two hit by the truck.

"There's no way Mykel's the primary target, so that's where we'll begin. I'll get our detectives to work tracking the killer. Don't worry, my department will locate and capture whoever did this. We'll find this son of a bitch. Trust me.

"Lt. Willcox is in charge of my team now. He'll complete your questioning. When he's finished, you won't be needed here any longer. We've got this now, my friend. You need to go to the M.E.'s office when you're done here."

Kyle shook his head. "No, Leo. Sorry. My staying here or going there won't bring her back. There'll be time enough for that. I've already begun my assessment. I have to keep going; that's how I work. I have to do this while the details are front and center. There's a bullet missing that needs to be found.

Standing where Mykel stood and pointing across the street, he said, "My guess is it probably ricocheted off the street, in that direction, and following that trajectory onto the parking lot."

"Okay, Kyle. I'll share that with Willcox. Now let my people do their job. You're on my witness list. I'll keep you posted on anything we find. Meantime, I'll want you to share any information you discover to Willcox. Promise me."

Kyle's eyes tried to burn a hole in the pavement when he uttered, "I'll try, Leo, but that's all I'm guaranteeing."

Willcox approached Kyle. He wore a stiff, synthetic smile, but everything from the neck down was on official business. "Sorry for your loss, Mr. McNally. Wish I didn't have to go over this with you now. I've assigned officers to find the slug. Tell me where you believe the shot or shots may have come from."

"There was just one shot. It came from behind and above them," and pointed to the parking garage two blocks south. "There was no second shot."

"Are you certain? Only a single shot?"

"Yes. The man behind Mykel was a head taller than her. He took a shot to the back of his head. It had to be a high velocity, jacketed round because it went through him and still entered and exited Mykel, center mass." Kyle turned, pointing again to the parking garage. "I'm certain that garage was the perfect spot for a shooter to set up, given my estimation of the trajectory. It would've given him good cover."

While Lt. Willcox finished jotting notes, Kyle stared blankly as the EMTs placed Mykel's body in the ambulance. "Oh, and Willcox, this wasn't a random shooting or a mass murder scenario."

"What makes you say that?"

"No wounded."

"Huh?"

"In all the mass shootings I've studied, there were other injured victims. No, I'm certain this was an assassination. Mykel's death wasn't planned. She was collateral damage."

Lt. Willcox completed his interview with Kyle and turned his attention to the team of officers working the area. The activity around the crime scene had become a cacophony of reverberating staccato noises with police radio transmissions, occasional sirens, horns honking, and shouted orders from the police.

Meanwhile, shaking and sweating, Kyle put on the clean shirt one of the first officers handed him. Now, he turned his attention to doing what he was trained to do.

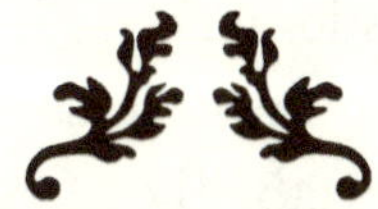

CHAPTER 21

IN THEIR INITIAL sweep, the investigating team didn't find the bullet. The man Kyle believed was the intended target was now identified as Felix Hermann from an ID. With that, Kyle recalled him as the person he'd run into yesterday in the offices of the Black Dragon Security Solutions Company.

He approached the medical examiner who was finishing his crime scene examination. "Excuse me doctor, anything to share with me about your initial findings?"

The examiner glanced at Kyle with one raised brow. He was a wizened senior with straggles of gray peppering his bushy brown hair, purple-rimmed baggy eyes, a scruffy mustache, and ears that could replace mudflaps on a Cadillac. "Hold your horses, buddy. How about we begin by you telling me who you are and giving me one good reason I should talk to you about anything?"

"My apologies, sir." Kyle held out his P.I. license. "I'm Kyle McNally, a private detective consulting with the Tampa police, on assignment with District Three's commander, Major Leo Davidson. The female victim you've examined is my fiancée, Mykel Hartley. Major Davidson asked me to work with his department on this investigation," Kyle lied.

"Sorry to hear that, McNally. But my rules are clear-cut. I'm required to report my findings directly to the homicide investigators working this case." The M.E. recognized the frustration on Kyle's face and offered him a crumb. "Outside of a cursory examination of the entry and exit wounds, the only test I've completed here is taking the liver and body temperatures. I'll know more after completing full autopsies back at the lab. Once I've got the ballistics report, I'll complete my report. If I'm told to rush it, I'd be done in the next day or two. But no promises."

Kyle cursed under his breath. The M.E. continued, "Mr. McNally, right now, my department's overtime workload is immense. Any escalation in priority needs to come from above. That's the only way this autopsy gets fast-tracked."

Thwarted, Kyle shook his head. He thanked the doctor and turned his attention back to the search for the missing slug. He joined the two officers already assigned there. Using a slow, grid pattern, they explored the path the bullet would've taken from where the bodies fell.

"Over here." One of the officers pointed to the slug, spotted lodged between a car tire and the pavement. A second officer began taking photos while the first one slipped on gloves, preparing to place it in an evidence bag.

AN HOUR LATER, the commotion around the crime scene had settled down. The ambulances were gone and only one of the police cars remained. Kyle returned his attention to the shooter's 'nest.' He walked the two blocks to the garage, stopping to survey the immediate area. Two squad cars, their lights flashing, were blocking the entrance, eliminating any ingress or egress. The food truck owners were documented and asked to leave the area.

Kyle noticed several homeless men sitting on benches, or sleeping behind them, in the park across the street.

He crossed the street and approached the nearest one, a man sitting with his trash bag of worldly goods beside him on the bench.

"Hello, mister. Got a minute?" The man lifted his arm to block the sun from his eyes and glanced left and right to confirm he wasn't being targeted by a prowling gang. He had a pale, pock-marked complexion, clear brown eyes, a long, hooked nose, tousled blonde hair, and a rust-colored beard. He wore a military jersey with a chevron patch on the shoulder embroidered with a red number one.

"Why? What d'ya want? I ain't done nothin'."

"No, no. I'm just hoping you'll spare me the time to answer a couple questions." He nodded and Kyle continued, "Okay if I sit?" pointing to the other end of the bench.

"I guess."

"I'd be happy to buy you a sandwich and coffee for your time." The man nodded, enthusiastically this time. "So, what's your name?"

The man scanned the park again for signs of danger. Seeing none, he turned back to Kyle. "Sal's the name, Sal Francisco. Sure, I could eat and have a cup of Joe. Just so there ain't no funny stuff involved. I don't roll that way—never have."

"No, Sal. No tricks. I promise. C'mon, let's get you that meal while we talk."

They sat at a table inside a sandwich shop across the street. Kyle ignored the other customer's nervous stares. "Sal, were sitting on that bench awhile?"

"Most of the morning. I come by here on Fridays because the food trucks setup around the block. On a good Friday, I usually manage to get a Cuban and a coffee; some do-gooder hoping to put points on their Karma board. No luck today though...not until you showed."

"You appear to have been a soldier, Sal. Am I right?" Kyle asked, pointing to the patch on his jacket.

He held up his hand while he took a deep pull on his coffee. "Yeah, I was a grunt in Vietnam for a year. Big Red One, north of Saigon. Walked point for my squad. Saw some real nasty shit there too; they even gave me a bronze star on account of a fire fight with some NVA regulars outside of Phu Loi. But damn, by the time I got back to the world, nothin' was the same. People changed. Acted like they were mad at me. I never got it."

"Neither did I. I was in high school when it ended. There was a lot of craziness back then. None of you vets deserved the treatment they got, Sal. My thanks for your service."

"I appreciate that. So, what's your name buddy?"

"Kyle. Kyle McNally."

"What d'ya want, Kyle?"

"You saw all the cop cars and ambulances down the street earlier. And they're searching the parking garage across the street now," he said, gesturing toward the police cars. "I'm wondering if you heard or saw anything unusual, a little more than an hour ago? Just before all the shit hit the fan?"

"Because I carry my world in a garbage sack, ya' know, sometimes I get targeted by some of the nastier creeps around here. I have to keep my jungle senses sharp."

"Jungle senses?"

"Yeah, when I was stationed in Nam busting through jungle on point, I had to keep my eyes constantly moving to spot any dangerous movement close by and those hidden, at a distance. I used my nose to pick up any unfamiliar smells, and my ears to listen for any telltale sounds. Saved my life and kept my squad safe for my entire tour," his face brightened as he continued, "got me the nickname, 'Radar.'"

"Every now and then, I still get a whiff of those jungles on a rainy day here. I'll never get the smell of napalm out of my nose; like burning gasoline and laundry soap together. Terrible, horrible stuff. Those are my bad days.

"And yeah, there was something earlier that made my senses snap to. Probably about the time you mentioned."

"What was it, Sal?"

"A single crack, sharp enough when it echoed off the buildings. I'm certain it came from that top floor there," he said, pointing to the parking garage. "Believe me, I know the sound of a rifle shot. It seemed suspicious, but with all the other shit going on around here, I didn't think nothin' more about it. At least not 'til a little while after."

"What happened then?"

"That's when this white van peels out of the garage. It had a sticker on the door that had a picture of a range target with the name of some construction outfit underneath. It got my attention because of the earlier shot. Like I say, I've always been good at connecting sights and sounds. Saved my bacon in Nam more than a couple times."

"You sure about the color of the van and the logo on the door?"

"Yep."

"I don't suppose you could ID the driver?"

"Couldn't pick him out in a crowd, but his window was down. He's a white guy with a thick beard, wearing a dark ball cap."

With a crooked smile, Kyle said, "I wonder if you caught the license plate?"

"Nah. Like I said, it didn't seem so important then, and the van was moving too fast anyway."

When the police cruisers pulled away from the garage, Kyle thanked Sal, handed him a folded twenty, and walked back to get his car.

KYLE STOOD ON the top floor of the garage, scribbling notes on a pad. Beyond several scratch marks on the concrete floor where the shooter's stand had been, he saw no other evidence. He'd check with Leo about anything the crime scene team found, and share what he'd learned from Sal.

Leaning against the low wall, eyes focuses on the intersection two blocks north, where, just hours earlier, he'd witnessed Mykel's murder. He stood transfixed, mesmerized by the horror of the scene he'd witnessed.

He now knew three things with absolute certainty. One: the shooter was a professional; two: he was hired to kill Felix Hermann; and three: he'd made a huge mistake. Killing Mykel was a mortal blunder. Kyle would personally escort this asshole to Hades.

CHAPTER 22

KYLE SLEPT SOUNDLY for about 30 minutes. Just after dawn, an explosive ring from his phone jolted him from his sleep. The rising winter sun tore through his curtains, blinding his right eye, while his mucous-glued left eye was grateful. In his sleep, he wrestled with shadows of guilt, remorse, and revenge; all while imagining a commensurate retribution for Mykel's killer. He turned over and growled. "What."

"Hey Kyle. It's Tony. Sorry for calling this early, but I haven't slept a wink since I learned about Mykel's murder. I mean, holy shit! Are you okay?"

Kyle threw the covers back and spat, "No, not by a mile. I'm not sure if I'll be able to sleep peacefully again. Right now, it feels like there's a shadow of me impersonating Kyle McNally," he said, eyes fixed on the side of the bed where Mykel should be.

"I can't begin to imagine, my friend. Is there anything you need me to do for you? Anyone you'd like me to contact up here? Anything at all?"

Kyle sat up and threw his legs over the side of the bed. "Nah. Don't think so Tony. I've covered as much as I'm able to for now. Patrick's meeting me at police headquarters this morning. He may have some ideas about the shooter."

"Okay then, if you're sure there's nothing for me to do from here, I'll see you tomorrow."

"Thanks, Tony. I swear to God, when I'm finished with him, he'll wish he'd never left his damned mother's womb."

CHAPTER 23

KYLE AND HIS father Patrick entered the Tampa Police headquarters at nine o'clock that morning. Major Davidson met them at his office door. "Come in Kyle. Hello Patrick. I wish we were meeting under different circumstances. The last time I spoke with you Patrick, we were trading shots at Chicago's Green Door Tavern on St. Patty's Day, wasn't it?

"Aye, Leo, though my recollection of that celebration is a bit misty."

"Would either of you like a cup of coffee, or tea, Patrick?"

"Yes, I'd take a cup of tea if you've got somethin' better than that commercial sludge they put in those tiny paper sacks." Taking a quick whiff of the air, Kyle declined.

When the three were seated, Kyle spoke first. "Anything new on Mykel's murder?"

There was a knock on the door, and Lt. Willcox stepped in. "Come in Nick." Then to Kyle and Patrick, "I've asked Nick to join us as he was the detective-in-charge at the scene." Willcox took a seat.

Davidson shifted in his chair and scowled at the case folder on his desk. "Not as much as I'd like, Kyle."

Leo began tapping his fingers on the table, then stopping and lifting his gaze, he left one finger pointing at Willcox. Willcox cleared his throat and spoke to Kyle. "I'm so very sorry for your loss, Kyle. Here's what we've learned so far. The shot that killed Mykel and Felix Hermann was a heavy bullet, full metal jacket. Our forensic team confirmed it came from a .338 Magnum cartridge, likely fired from a military-style sniper rifle. It's a high velocity round that entered and exited both victims before landing where it was found. There was no shell casing in the garage, and we found precious little other evidence. I wish we had more.

"What we have now are photos of tire tracks and faint footprints, but we're not sure if they're the shooter's yet. We can't create a composite of him as there were no eyewitnesses. The witness you spoke with, Kyle, Sal Francisco's account didn't give us much more to work with other than his recognition of a shot and vague description of his vehicle. We're searching state and national VINs for a possible match."

Kyle spoke up, "Did you contact the Bank of America for perimeter video footage? It's right across the street from the garage. Or any other neighborhood commercial stores to check for cameras?"

"Our team checked with the bank and were told there was a network glitch their techs are troubleshooting. So, they've got nothing for us. And, no luck with the other nearby businesses," Leo said.

"I agree with your initial conclusion Kyle. This guy's a serious pro who we believe exited the garage within fifteen minutes of the shooting. If it took him a couple minutes longer to setup the nest, then our time frame places him moving in shortly after eleven and out by one-fifteen."

Patrick leaned in and said, "I've got a couple notions I'm tossing. This perp's efficiency brings to mind a contractor that appeared on our radar while I was still with Interpol. As told, this fella trained as a sniper with the British army. Sometime in the mid-eighties, name of Cross, if I remember right. I'm waitin' for more info from my contacts at ICPO."

Leo asked, "Was he good?"

"Uh huh. One o' the best. He made his reputation in Iraq during Desert Storm. His regiment gave him the nickname, *Dire*; named his rifle *Dire Fate*. He's said to have gotten over fifty kills during his tour. Since leaving the military, he's gotten high marks as an assassin for hire."

Leo jumped in. "If this guy's our shooter, he's used his military training to become a contract killer who takes credit cards now?"

"And I'll bet there's someone here in Tampa who paid him to kill Hermann," Kyle suggested. "I'll continue following this lead with Patrick."

Leo leaned forward in his chair. "If Patrick is right, Kyle, then let's begin by working backwards from there to determine who would stand to profit from his death. Patrick, are you aware if this man's worked here in the states before?"

"No. Not from nothin' I heard before I left Interpol. I'll keep the lines open with my former team there to keep up with any recent news on the bloke."

"Anything you need me to do on my end Patrick? Anyone I can contact?" Leo said.

"Not yet."

Kyle shook his head and rose to leave.

CHAPTER 24

KYLE DROVE SOUTH on Bayshore Boulevard just after noon. He'd awakened thinking it was Sunday, and he still wasn't sure. His mind was short-circuiting. He struggled with a recent recurring dream of being stuck in a subway station where all the destinations were written in a language he didn't know.

On his way to an appointment with Jolene Papadapolis, for the first time in memory, Kyle couldn't marshal his thoughts. With Mykel's funeral only two days away, there'd been no updates from either Patrick or Leo about her slaying. He needed to get moving on his investigation into the Y2K serial killer, but his typically structured, analytical brain was AWOL. Kyle couldn't recall a time when he'd felt this untethered. He was pissed at himself, pissed at his life, and pissed at the world. *Wake up McNally! Remember, 'Holding onto rage is like drinking rat poison and expecting the rat to die' You're not gonna die today!*

The local Chamber of Commerce advertised Bayshore Boulevard as the longest continuous sidewalk in the world. No other metropolis had contested that claim. When he pulled into the Papadapolis' driveway, he was in front of one of the stateliest mansions in a row of impressive personal monuments to success and wealth Tampa offered. The front veranda ran the length of the home, and an ornamental gazebo overlooked

Hillsborough Bay. If you were rich, socially aspirational, and living in Tampa, this is where you dropped anchor.

"Good morning, Kyle," Jolene said, with a sweep of her hand showing him in.

"Hello Jo. Quite a place you've got here," then smiling, "I'll bet you keep a map handy to find all the rooms."

She laughed, "Yes, but it's the easy-to-read kind, with bright colored arrows and a legend. Would you like a cup of coffee, or, maybe something stronger?"

"No, thank you."

When they were seated on the covered back veranda overlooking an Olympic-sized swimming pool with a built-in hot tub and jacuzzi, Jolene said, "So, what have you learned about the danger to me Kyle?"

"I spoke with my friend at the Tampa police. After checking the accident report the officers filed, he confirmed it was long on supposition and short on procedure. Once they measured your blood alcohol level at .06, their attention appeared to focus solely on your intoxication, neglecting any further site investigation. And, after reviewing the police photos of your car, it was apparent you weren't speeding.

"You told me the vehicle that forced you off the road struck your car?"

"Yeah, it did. He bumped into me. On instinct, I veered right, trying to avoid a crash, and that's when I hit the tree."

Kyle straightened and said, "So, you believe it was a man who forced you off the road?"

"Yeah, I guess it was. Sorry, I've been confused some recently. Events seem to blur together; I don't know why."

Kyle's jaw tightened and he shifted back in his seat. *That's not what she told me the other day.*

"When I mentioned it to the police, I was told the officers reported no signs of a recent side impact on your car. And, there was nothing in their report about your identifying a male driving the other car. So, I'd like take a look at your car before I leave." *Her story is changing.*

"I visited the scene of the accident on my way here. The city crews are busy with the damage from Hurricane Marcos and they hadn't re-sodded the area yet. I inspected the site and the damaged tree. There was a single set of tire tracks leaving the road. I also found a half-buried automobile badge in one of the tire tracks. It's from a late model Ford. I'll take it to the police forensic team for confirmation."

"Well, that seals it. Those idiots! If they'd pulled their heads out of their asses, they'd have found the badge that night. I damn sure never thought much of cops before, but, by God, now I know why." Jolene, now shaking visibly, began wringing her hands. She stood and said, "Please excuse me Kyle, but I'm gonna need a moment to pull myself together. Please wait. Could I get you that cup of coffee now?"

"Yes, thank you Jo."

Leaving her composure behind, she walked from the room. Sounds from the kitchen included the sound of a pill bottle being upended on the kitchen counter. He shook his head. *This case is gonna be tougher than I thought.*

Kyle scanned the pastoral scene beyond the pool deck. Statuesque Italian pines lined the property on all sides. Midway between the deck and the back property line was a massive water fountain. The foundation was snowy marble, and a life-sized bronze mermaid held a large conch shell above her head. Four smaller, white marble dolphins directed jets inward. *'Other half'* crossed his mind. Followed by, *I hope she doesn't have that astrology chart she talked about making for me.*

Jolene returned with an etched silver service with a sweetly aromatic, caramel-fragranced Jamaican coffee. An impish smile gave away her improved mood. After placing a notebook on the table in front of him, she poured his coffee.

"So, Kyle, what's our next move?"

"I spoke with Gabby Rostock; she claims there's no animosity toward you from her, or the group. She says they're all just worried about you."

"Oh, really? Do you believe she was telling the truth?"

"Yes, I do. And, as soon as Tony Petrocelli joins me at Paladin, he'll begin shadowing you. We'll schedule that service for a couple weeks. Whenever you leave your house, he'll be close by. If he sees any suspicious activity, he'll pursue it. Meantime, I'll stay in touch with the police in case they come up with more information about your car crash."

"Thank you, Kyle. That's a relief. These troubles have been circling my head like vultures lately." Then, with slumped shoulders and downcast eyes, "that, and my problems with Dom; over the past couple months… well…uh…no, never mind, that's a story for another day. I'm just praying you'll find those people out to get me."

Kyle leaned back when her face lit up and she blurted, "But, I'd like to share the birth chart I prepared for you. What d'ya say? It might be fun! Who knows, you may learn something about yourself. We all have secrets…and they're almost always ones we keep from others, *and* ourselves."

The sudden change of mood surprised him. And now, her face wore a playful grin as she expectantly looked at him.

He flashed a supportive smile as he glanced at his watch. "Well… sure Jo, I guess I'm okay with it," wondering if she'd tell him something that'd help him sleep better.

"I promise to make this short."

"Thanks."

"You, Kyle McNally, are a Scorpio. Scorpio is a feminine water sign, meaning you're self-contained and have strong inner reserves. You value your privacy and are close with very few people. You possess a strong imagination and don't like routine. You have an excellent memory, an imaginative mind, and common sense.

"You're a man who lives in two worlds. On the one hand, you are a detached, independence-loving introvert. On the other, you're drawn to the shiny things of the world, like love, sex, recognition, and material comforts. I also read you as a man of honor who, unfortunately, lives in a world which cares little for such virtues. A pity."

She leaned in smiling, and with a wink said, "How'm I doing so far, Kyle?"

"Not bad. Not bad at all Jo. Though that 'man of honor' part reminds me of some kind of knight sitting at a round table. Don't think I'll ever be mistaken for that guy."

"You prefer working alone because, often, working with other's input only slows you down. Obviously, you don't mind being called a lone wolf.

"You are good at disguising your moods. In your personal relationships, you always pursue perfection in others, gravitating only to those who are driven like you, and intellectual equals. Anyone else is disappointing, and discarded.

"There's more, but I promised to keep this short. What d'ya think?"

Kyle sat back with a relaxed smile and said, "Jo, I'm surprised at your evaluation. It was very insightful. Thank you."

"Well, now I'm confident you are the right person to help get me out of this mess," Jolene said.

He stood and reached for the leather-bound booklet she offered. Its heft surprised him.

"I'm glad you like it. We can talk more about it after you read it. More than a few people have told me I have a gift for interpreting charts."

"Thank you, Jo. I've got to be going. Please pull your car out of the garage. I'd like to check the fender and take a few pictures. It'd be nice if I could find more that may have been missed."

CHAPTER 25

WHEN HE SAW the number on his ringing phone, he tensed.

"Hello?"

"Tell me you had nothing to do with this."

He frowned. "We agreed that calling me here is a bad idea."

"Never mind that."

He sat back and oozed, "*Okay, I'll bite*. Nothing to do with what?"

"The murder."

He straightened. "The what!?"

"When we spent those nights together, I told you he was planning to leave the company."

He clawed one hand through his hair. "C'mon, don't be ridiculous. What in the name of sweet Jesus gave you such a preposterous notion?"

"Just answer me!"

"No, absolutely not. Nothing to do with it."

CHAPTER 26

THE RECEPTIONIST DIRECTED Kyle to Dominic Papadapolis' office at Black Dragon Security Solutions Company. On the way, Kyle's attention was diverted to one of the offices he passed. Its shelves were decorated with dozens of model characters, likely from the Dungeons and Dragons milieu. An odd-looking character sat at the desk, furiously typing on his keyboard. He wore a sparkling blood-red turban, blue-tinted, wire-rimmed sunglasses, and sported a Van Dyke style mustache with goatee, waxed and twisted up hipster style. He reminded Kyle of a character from the cover of the Beatles,' 'Sgt. Pepper's Lonely Hearts Club Band.' Kyle smiled as he stepped into Dom's office. *Must be casual Friday.*

"Hello again Kyle," Dom said. "Come in."

"Hello Dom."

"I'm glad you came now. I'm just finishing preparations for overseas meetings this weekend."

With a bemused smile, Kyle said, "I have to ask about the man I saw on my way in. He missed Halloween by a week. Does he usually work dressed like a royal prince from 'One Thousand and One Nights?'"

"No, no. That's Scott Kaine, head of our software development teams. He does that once a week, on random days. Most days he dresses less curiously. An interesting fellow. Never met a mirror he didn't love.

Super bright, possibly a savant, but comes complete with a team of over-caffeinated monkeys under that turban.

"But please, tell me how your meeting with Jo went." Then, with a slow building smile and a wink, Dom leaned forward and said, "I'll bet she hit you up with an astrology chart, didn't she?"

"Yes, she did. And, actually, it surprised me."

"She does that with everyone she meets. Between you and me, Jo's an angel on her knees, but can be a devil on her feet. Seriously though, any progress on the case of her car accident or her mysterious stalkers? I hope this isn't too much nonsense for you. Of course, I'll pay you for all your billable hours. But, please let her down easy when you come up empty with her ghosts."

Kyle steadied his gaze. "Actually, Dom, I've found some validity to her story about the car crash. When I visited the site, I found a car badge near the accident. It was half-buried in tire tracks. It's from a Ford. The officers apparently missed it in their rush to pin her with a DUI. And I have photos of a small blue paint mar on the left front bumper of her car. It gives additional credence to her claim she was forced off the road.

"My friend at TPD is taking this evidence to their lab techs for follow-up. Hopefully, they'll determine how recent the scrape was, the make and model of the car the badge came from, and whether the paint sample matches factory colors.

"In the meantime, I'll be providing temporary surveillance for Jolene to confirm or refute her beliefs she's being followed. She's happy with that arrangement."

"Well, it may be just a waste of time, but follow this if you must, Kyle. As I told you before, if anything were to happen to Jolene, it'd crush me."

CHAPTER 27

SATURDAY, NOVEMBER THIRTEENTH, at the Woodlawn Cemetery in north Ybor City, a small group of friends moved away from Mykel Hartley's gravesite. The internment ceremony, conducted by the pastor from the very church where they'd intended to marry, was concluded.

An unseasonably warm, southwesterly breeze drifted between the headstones on a darkly overcast mid-November day. The air carried the fragrance of freshly mown grass and warm, sandy earth. Hurricane Marcos had left a merciless path of mayhem through central Florida less than two weeks ago.

Wearing dark sunglasses, Kyle stood over Mykel's grave, his face telegraphing his black mood. From the set of his jaw, and the clenched, white-knuckled fists, there was no disguising the red-hot rage roiling just beneath the surface.

He slipped a piece of paper from his pocket and mouthed the words, *'Death leaves a heartache no one can heal. Love leaves a memory no one can steal.'* Those words were inscribed on his mother's headstone years ago in Ireland, when he was fourteen and witnessed her violent murder. It would be engraved on Mykel's as well. The tragedies of both his mother's and Mykel's savagely violent deaths were bound forever now.

A shadow of a smile passed over Kyle's face, belying the tearful eyes that revealed the truth of his profound despair. He whispered, "I love you Mykel… you're taking my heart with you."

He knelt and dug a shallow hole with his fingers in the soft sand before the gravestone. There he placed a never-to-be-worn gold wedding band before covering it. He turned and walked to his car where his friend and partner, Tony Petrocelli, waited.

THE FUNERAL GUESTS had left. Kyle, Tony, and Patrick sat silently on the condo balcony for an hour. Strains of Vivaldi's *The Four Seasons* violin concerto intoned softly on the radio. Kyle blankly stared through his snifter of Grand Marnier; Tony gripped a bottle of Michelob tight enough to shatter it; and Patrick sat, head lowered with elbows braced on his knees, holding an iced glass of 30-year-old Slane whiskey to his forehead. A chance breeze carried the citrus and jasmine scent of Mykel's favorite Chanel perfume from an open bedroom window. Tears coursed down Kyle's cheeks.

Tony broke the silence. "Damn it Kyle! How in the name of God could this happen? For Christ's sake, today was supposed to be your wedding day."

Kyle's jaw muscles clenched. "In the name of God? For Christ's sake?" Kyle, face, frozen in pain, mumbled, "None of that matters today, Tony. She's gone.

"Is there an answer? Maybe, but it's not coming from any world religions, the great philosophers, or any of the myriad pop-up prophets and charlatans claiming to have *the truth* about life and death. If God exists, it's not the one preached about in churches, written about in books, or hustled by politicians."

He paused, and with half-closed eyes shook his lowered head before continuing. "So, what's the alternative? What if we're just an experiment started by a cruel alien species living light years from us? I can imagine them bent over, laughing and slapping their knees, as they observe our continuous chaos and endless compulsion for collective suicide.

"Or, what if we're just simple sport for them, like a Saturday baseball game, Cubs battling the Sox, or in millennia past, the Huns swarming the Romans.

"What if our planet is just a giant experimental, astronomical ant farm, and these fun-loving aliens hoist it up and shake it every couple of thousand years or so. Given the current state of the world, is that impossible to imagine?

"Or, that they've spent these past four or five millennia trying to perfect us?" His voice cracking, "Because if that was their intention, then we can all agree they're doing a pretty shitty job, right?"

When Kyle paused, Tony slowly shook his head and said, "I'm so sorry."

"Mykel's gone. Right now, all I'm feeling is an incredible rage. My heart and my bed are both cold. I'm empty. 'Memento mori' is a warning, one with a painful cost; one Mykel paid without consenting."

Patrick leaned forward and spoke. "Sadly, I gonna' agree. Tony, I too am Catholic. When you tally my many mistakes and toss in my violent career with Interpol, my faith's been sorely tested. I read somewhere that without knowin' pain, we'd never feel love or appreciate beauty.

"And I do understand how ya feel, Kyle. God's my witness, I wish I'd of done better by you back when yer mother was remorselessly killed. I'll likely pay fer it when I'm no longer on the green side o' the grass. So, though 'tis sad for me, I'll pardon your cynicism.

"It seems in this hard world, we McNally men are fated to lose the women we love most. Tis a damnable price to pay. But Mykel is now safe, in a place of peace, and it's left to us who remain to deal with her passing. And deal with it, we will. There's an Irish proverb I'm reminded of, '*The place where there is sorrow, solace comes with it.*'

"May the three of us vow here and now to seek solace in avenging her death." All three raised and tapped their glasses.

Too Late for Hope, That Time's Past.
Y2K Is Here!
You Know This Won't Be My Last —
Don't Guess Who I Am, Just Ask.

- Y2K

CHAPTER 28

CUSCADAN PARK WAS renowned years back for professional baseball stars like Lou Piniella, Dave Magadan, and Al·Lopez; up-and-coming boxers Matt Perfitti and Sixto Morales; and a unique two story above-ground Bintz swimming pool. The pool closed a few years back, when city leaders gave up trying to fix the many leaks.

I like parks. They suit my needs. I cruise it slowly and park two blocks away on Holmes Avenue. My target is hunched on the first row of the bleachers facing the ball field.

Poor fool. Just one more of the many losers, loners, and low-lifes. They are the barnacles clinging to society's pylons. I am the slayer; gotta scrape 'em all off.

A pale, intermittently blinking street lamp does a poor job of illuminating the field. I creep from tree to tree until I am within twenty feet of him. He still doesn't notice me. I'm ten feet away when I stop and say, "Hello, Todd?"

He jumps unsteadily from his seat and shouts, "Wha-wha…what! Who are you?" His speech is slurred and his hands are shaking.

Now I'm eight feet in front of him and I repeat, "Todd?"

"Who the hell is Todd?"

Four feet from him, I pretend confusion, saying, "Look buddy, I'm sorry. I'm here to meet a guy named Todd."

"I'm not Todd. Leave me alone! I ain't botherin' nobody."

"My mistake mister. I met this guy, Todd, earlier today and he told me to meet him here tonight. We were goin' to hook up, ya know?"

"Please go. I got here first. Ya hear me? Just get outta here."

"Look, I'm really sorry about the mistake mister. Let me make it up to you," I say, reaching into my left jacket pocket. "Here, I've got a five-dollar bill and a ticket for a free Cuban sandwich from that bakery over on Fifteenth. What d'ya say? Just give me a chance to make it up to you."

"I guess. Okay," he said, holding his hand out.

I take a step forward, withdraw the switchblade from the right jacket pocket and press the release slide. With the sudden sharp click-click of the knife, the degenerate's eyes grow wide and his mouth falls open. Thrusting powerfully, my first strike comes from the right, severing his trachea, followed by a second one, backhanded from the left, which nicks his right carotid artery.

I take three steps back, watching as my prey struggles for breath, with his lifeblood spraying over the ground. In hopeless desperation, he writhes, first to the left and then to the right. But his struggles are ending. First, his knees buckle and he twists and collapses onto his side. Then I'm surprised when, with a last spasm, he flips over on his back… never saw that before. I study his face, confirming the excellence and righteousness of my judgement. I consider his sentence justly imposed. My work here is finished.

I saunter back to my car, whistling Led Zepplin's 'Your Time Is Gonna Come.'

CHAPTER 29

AT THREE P.M., Kyle joined a meeting in progress at Major Davidson's office at police headquarters. Lt. Willcox, Sgt. Dallas, and Cpl. O'Shea were all seated around a table, not a single smile among them. Kyle noticed an array of gruesome photographs spread on the table.

"Sorry to call you in today, Kyle," Leo said, "but there's been another Y2K killing. This one happened in Cuscadan Park last night. And, a new poem was dropped at the Trib's office."

He passed the copied file to Kyle, who took a moment to consider it and inspect the photographs. "The team's been there all morning searching for clues and witnesses. The M.E. confirmed a couple of details. He says the assailant is right-handed, based on the slash patterns from both of the last two vics. Same double-edged-style knife; the wound on the front of his neck, sliced the trachea, is deeper than the one on the right which severed the carotid artery. He also estimates the attacker's height at about six feet from the angle of the cuts. But, that's all we've got so far."

Kyle asked the obvious, "Did the killer leave any physical evidence?"

"Very little. And no fingerprints on the letter either."

"What time did it take place?"

"Best the M.E. can give us, it likely occurred between ten and twelve o'clock."

"Did your techs find any prints on the ground?"

"Yes, but unfortunately, there were several sets. We're searching the federal databases now."

"There's a lot of blood on the ground around the vic. Have they tested for type?"

"They did. But the victim's is the only type confirmed."

"I'm sure the neighbors have been questioned."

Sergeant Dallas spoke up, "Yes, they have, Mr. McNally. No one reported anything before, during, or after our time window."

Kyle grimaced. "Sergeant, were you able to contact *all* the nearby neighbors?"

"No, we had several who weren't home. I've made a list of those we spoke with."

"Major, any problem with my going to the crime scene? Or, speaking with the missed neighbors myself?"

Staring directly at Lt. Willcox, the major tilted his head slightly and said, "Nick?"

Glaring back at Davidson, Willcox muttered, "So this is how it's gonna to be? This guy's gonna second-guess our work, and backstop us from now on? I don't—"

Davidson cut him off. "Nick, this operation isn't about who's a better detective. We've got two confirmed murders by this Y2K creep, and two previous ones that fit his M.O. before these poems started showing up. We've got to locate and capture this killer quickly. And," slamming his fist on the table, "God damnit, I mean before one more indigent vic turns up in our city parks.

"I shouldn't need to remind you we've got a murder/homicide rate here in Tampa that's twice the national average. So, yes, this department will take all the help we can get.

"Kyle's professional expertise is one possible answer. But, believe me, I'm going to continue reaching out in all directions until this case is solved. I don't care if I have to hire a damn psychic! It's not *your* reputation Nick; it's that of the entire force."

Dallas and O'Shea shifted in their seats, avoiding eye contact as Willcox replied. "Sorry sir. It's just, well, I'm not comfortable with anyone peering over my shoulder. Especially not a civilian."

Glaring at Willcox with narrowed eyes, Davidson said, "Well, Nick, until you come to me with better intel to give the chief and the mayor, get used to it."

O'Shea hesitantly spoke up. "Sorry Nick, but I'm gonna agree with the major. We need all the help we can get on this case. This Y2K perp is a clever son of a bitch. He's dodged us so far. Let's be patient and cooperate. If McNally can help us find this guy, more's the better. He's got a proven record." Dallas nodded.

Willcox shook his head again before answering. "Well, I'm damn sure not going to fight my team over this. For now, I'll keep my mouth shut."

"Putting any disagreements aside then, let's consider this new 'poem' and try to figure out what it means," Leo said, pointing to where he'd written it on the whiteboard.

'Too Late for Hope, That Time's Past. Y2K Is Here! You Know This Won't Be My Last – Don't Guess Who I Am, Just Ask–Y2K.'

"Team, any ideas?"

"Outside of the challenge, he's reaffirming that it's some kind of messianic mission for him," O'Shea said.

Kyle nodded. "I agree. He's using a biblical, end-of-days comparison to this media-driven notion that on January 1st, 2000, the financial world will collapse and send us all back into the dark ages. That also explains the Y2K, or 'Year 2000,' moniker. It's the delusion of a madman.

"And I believe his closing challenge contains a clue. The two words, 'Just Ask,' are likely a hint to his identity. He imagines he's being clever, but I'll bet the word 'Ask' is significant and may be an acronym pointing to the author's identity."

"How's that sound, Nick?" Leo asked.

"Couldn't this be a copycat?"

"Not likely since the first two murders were kept out of the papers," Leo replied.

Nick continued, "Okay, and though the word 'ask' as a clue is plausible, I guess, but how do we run with that? Seems pretty thin to me. Should I devote my team's attention to the word 'ask?'"

Davidson looked to Kyle. "What about it?"

"A nickname? Maybe, but my first instinct is it's his initials."

Nick slowly shook his head and spat, "So, is it your idea we should go to the phonebook and find everyone in the city of Tampa having those initials?"

Leo broke in, "Easy Nick. It sounds like a simplistic idea, but right now, it's the only one on our plate."

Kyle jumped in, "And, unfortunately, there's the possibility the initials might not be in a proper order, so we'll need to check for variations in the letter order: in case *a-s-k* doesn't pan out."

"Any other suggestions?" Leo said. He paused momentarily, searching their faces for a response; getting none, he said, "I'm assigning our techs to an electronic directory search in Tampa first, and expand it to Hillsborough County if needed."

"Nick, go wait in my office. *Immediately.*"

BEFORE LEO ROSE to leave, Kyle asked him about visiting the park.

"Sure, but I insist you take Corporal O'Shea with you. I want police presence in and around any of these crime scenes." Catching Kyle's grimace, he cautioned, "Don't make me remind you of the conditions of our agreement."

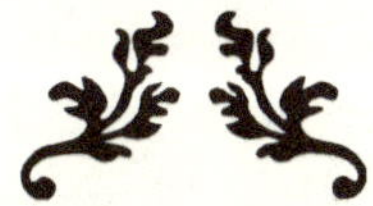

CHAPTER 30

ON THE ROAD to Cuscadan Park, Kyle's observations of Corporal Shannon O'Shea included her nearly perpetual smile away from headquarters. She stood five-feet, seven inches tall, sported bobbed auburn hair, and had fascinating green eyes with gold flecks. He guessed her to be mid-twenties, and she possessed a proud bearing accompanied by an eye-catching figure.

"When did you join the force, corporal?"

"They hired me in 1995. I'd just ended my academy training and got lucky when Tampa hired me. They were my first choice."

"It was the same when I went to work with the Chicago police. Have you always lived in the Tampa area?"

"Yep, born and raised nearby in Lutz, just north of the city; pretty much just a cow town back then. How about you?"

"Born in Staten Island, New York. Mother married and took me to Ireland with my stepfather. I returned stateside and finished my academy training before relocating to Chicago, where I got the best job offer. After twenty years with them, I'd had enough; decided it was time to settle down in the sunshine state, go private, and open up my own business."

"Interesting. A bit more international than my story…I like it! So where do you want to begin this morning? Gotta plan?"

"Let's start at the park; maybe we'll find something there. The crime scene is sixteen hours old, O'Shea, but there's been no rain. It's possible we'll find something forensics missed."

"Doesn't sound like you have faith in our team."

"No, that's not it. In my experience, forensic people get as over-whelmed by their caseloads as law enforcement. And that pressure can result in a rushed sweep of the site. I get it. They're human too. Honestly, I doubt if we'll find anything new, but it's one of those 'if we don't check, we'll never be sure' situations. After, let's see if we can find any of the neighbors missed this morning. We'll work from the list of residents Dallas made."

THEIR EXAMINATION OF Cuscadan Park turned up no new evidence. Kyle and O'Shea were going door-to-door now, seeking information from anyone who may have noticed something the previous night. A couple of those interviewed said they'd already spoken with the police and were concerned about the second visit. O'Shea assured them it was normal police procedure.

They'd covered most of the homes along North 15th Street, and north Avenida de Cuba, and were now visiting homes on Holmes Avenue. Most of the residences were one- and two-story bungalows, typical of a former middle-class neighborhood in Ybor with few garages and an occasional car parked in the yard.

They finished canvasing the north side of the street and were work-ing their way east from 12th Street, back toward the park. At the third house, they knocked and a young Hispanic woman answered. She stood about five-feet tall, with wavy, jet-black hair tied in a pony tail, and brown, almond-shaped eyes. Seeing Corporal O'Shea in uniform, her posture stiffened and her eyes darted side to side to see if anyone else was with them.

"Hello?" she said, beneath questioning brows.

Presenting her identification, O'Shea said, "Hello ma'am. I'm Corporal Shannon O'Shea with the Tampa Police Department, and this is Kyle McNally, a private investigator working with us. We are gathering information concerning the murder of a man last night in the park down the street. We'd like to ask you a few questions, if we may." Children's happy shrieks came from inside, accompanied by the rise and fall of raucous TV programming. The aroma of cumin seasoned ground beef and butter-sautéed vegetables drifted through the doorway.

"My mother told me the police came by earlier today, but she knew nothing of the man who was murdered. I don't know if I'd be much help. I work a full-time job and attend part-time evening classes at USF. I only learned about the murder as I was leaving my job. Such a tragedy. Poor man."

"May we please come in? I promise, we'll only need a few minutes of your time."

"Yes, of course. Please come in."

"For the record, may I ask your name and who else lives here with you?" O'Shea asked, opening her notepad.

"Maria Martinez. I live here with my mother, Arsenia De Santos, and my two children."

Ms. Martinez shooed the children to their room and turned off the TV. When they were seated, Kyle asked, "Did you know the murdered man, Ms. Martinez? We've been told he went by the name Vincent or Vinny."

"No, not personally, though I saw him on our street occasionally. As I say, I'm away from the house weekdays and two nights a week, so he could've been around more."

"Did you ever speak with him?" Kyle said.

"No, but I thought he was a nice man because whenever he noticed me, he would smile and give a quick wave."

"Were you at home last night, Ms. Martinez?" O'Shea said.

"Yes. But only after I got home from my nursing class at the university."

"Did you notice anything unusual between about ten o'clock and midnight?" O'Shea said.

She considered the question before answering. "Nothing much. This neighborhood is pretty quiet on Mondays this time of year. That's when I put the trash cans on the street."

"Did you notice anything different on the street last night?" Kyle asked.

"Well, there was a new car parked a couple doors down. One I don't remember seeing around here before…but that's not all that unusual."

Taking out her notepad, Corporal O'Shea asked, "Could you describe it?"

"Sure. It was a dark blue Ford Escort with four doors. I believe it was a 1993 to 1995 model."

"That's surprisingly specific, Ms. Martinez. How can you be so sure about the make and model years?" Kyle asked.

"My father was an auto mechanic. He owned a successful garage on 22nd Street. I worked part time for him from the time I learned to twist a socket wrench. Bless his heart, he didn't pay me, but I enjoyed our conversations about American cars and how their engineering and build quality had fallen behind the Europeans.

"And I also know when Ford changed the Escort's body style between '93 and '95. They changed the finish on the door handles and painted them to match the body color. That makes them easy to pick out from other models."

Grinning, O'Shea said, "I don't suppose you caught the license number, did you?"

"No, sorry. Didn't catch it."

O'Shea jotted her final notes, glanced up, and said, "Thank you Ms. Martinez, you've been very helpful. Please keep our cards. We may get back with you if we need to, but in the meantime, please call me if you recollect anything else."

Walking back to the car, O'Shea said, "I'll get with the license bureau on that car's make and model number. There shouldn't be all that many in the Tampa area, right?"

Kyle shot O'Shea a wry smile. "I love your optimism, O'Shea," before adding, "and that was an excellent interview. Glad you were there."

KYLE GOT BACK to his office after 9 p.m., poured himself four fingers of Maker's Mark, and collapsed at his desk. With a deep sigh, he took a big swallow. The bracing, complex aromas of the bourbon held charred-oak-barrel caramel, vanilla, toasted nuts, and spice fragrances, only elevated his flagging state of mind a little. This was the time of day when he missed Mykel most.

He placed a call to Jolene Papadapolis. "Hello Jo. I hope I'm not calling too late."

"No no. I'm never in bed before midnight unless there's a man waiting." Then. with slurred speech, she cackled, "N-no, not at all."

"Good. I'm calling to ask if tomorrow's a good day to bring my partner, Tony Petrocelli, over to meet you. I'd like to introduce him, and arrange for your shadowing. Would nine o'clock be okay?"

"Sure Kyle. I'm relieved you're sticking with me on this. Dom hasn't been home for the past couple nights. 'Out traveling,' he says…probably rev-v-v-ving his engines for divorce, that bastard." Kyle noted the anguish in her unsteady voice.

"Sorry to hear it, Jo. I hope you're mistaken. Try to get some rest. We'll be by tomorrow."

Kyle poured himself another four fingers of golden Novocain before reaching out to Tony.

"Hey Tony."

"Hi Kyle. What's up?"

"I just got off the phone with Jolene Papadapolis. She agreed to meet with us in the morning at nine. We'll iron out the conditions of your shadow with her then."

"Great. It'll be good to get back to work with you. And, I've found an apartment. I'm signing the lease day after tomorrow.

"Good news, Tony."

"So, are you coming back to your condo tonight?"

"No. I'm gonna sleep here."

"That makes three nights running, Kyle. Are you sure you're okay?—anything you need?"

"Nah, the couch here is comfortable. Thanks. I suppose this'll get easier with time. I've just got a lot to work through, right now."

"I hear you, Kyle. But if you want to talk about anything, I'll be here, okay?"

"Thanks Tony. I'll be by early to get cleaned up and change clothes before we head over to Joanne's. I'll catch up with you in the morning."

"Roger that, Kyle."

Kyle pressed his head between his hands, fingers massaging his scalp. These past two weeks had been a blur. Mykel's death had shredded his peace of mind. He hadn't gotten a good night's sleep and was uncomfortable going back to their condominium; too many reminders of a future that was a mirage now. He fell asleep at his desk, head resting uneasily on his arms.

CHAPTER 31

H**ER HAIR A** mess, eyes bloodshot, and mumbling something about the hour, Jolene Papadapolis opened her front door. Tony's eyes were fixed on her dressing gown, or rather, its state. The front was open, revealing a scanty burgundy-silk underclothing set, with a lace-trimmed camisole top and matching bottoms. There was no missing her arresting physique.

Nonplussed, Kyle said, "Hello Jo. I mentioned I'd introduce you to my partner at the agency, Tony Petrocelli. He'll be providing your security over the next couple weeks."

Straitening, she scanned him up and down slowly, and said, "Nice to meet you Mr. Tony." And winking at Kyle, "You didn't tell me he's such a looker, Kyle.

"I haven't surprised you, have I?"

"No, no. Just late rising. Tony, I insist you call me Jo."

He swallowed hard, reluctantly trying to re-establish eye contact before reaching out to shake her hand. "Pleasure to meet you, Jo."

"C'mon in and sit, boys," she said, standing aside, fumbling with a button on her gown. "Can I get either of you a cup of coffee?"

Both declined. Seated on her back patio, Tony said, "Jo, if I'm doing my job, you won't see me when I'm on duty. If you need to reach me, you'll have my cell number. I'll contact you immediately if I detect any suspicious activity nearby," Tony said.

"She will provide you with her daily schedule, Tony. Jo, since you told me you don't have any appointments or trips planned today, Tony will start work first thing tomorrow morning. He'll be available mornings and afternoons, based on your schedule."

"Thank you. Thank you both. Tony, I'm relieved that you'll be watching out for me over the next couple weeks. I'm sure you'll spot the creeps who've been following me. Hardly a day goes by when I don't notice them. Please stay in touch."

"I'll do that Jo."

SITTING IN THE Papadapolis driveway after their meeting, Tony whistled and said, "Damn Kyle, does she always dress like that for your appointments?"

"No, but she's always full of surprises. Don't let the loose talk fool you. Her hands were shaking bad, and her pupils were so big her eyes looked black. She's scared.

"Tony, I met with the Y2K team yesterday. Another homeless murder in a park. Same MO. The killer is picking up his pace. Corporal O'Shea and I visited the scene. Nothing there. But in an interview after, we picked up a useful lead. I'll keep you posted because I'm also planning to have you work with me on some nighttime reconnaissance. Leo says they've increased their coverage of the Ybor parks, but they're already stretched thin. I'm thinking two more sets of eyes might help."

"I'm ready, tell me when and where you need me."

"I also cleared it with Leo to meet with the wife of the sniper's target, Felix Hermann. I'm heading there now. She was interviewed by the Y2K team. They came away with no useful information, so I asked Leo for a chance to speak with her. He agreed, reluctantly, over Willcox's objections. I'm not convinced Willcox has either the patience or the skills. I'm hoping to uncover the motive, or motives, behind Hermann's murder. If I'm lucky, I'll catch something they missed."

"My money's on you."

"Let's meet for lunch at Sagua La Grande. I'll catch you up then."

CHAPTER 32

KYLE AND CORPORAL O'Shea arrived for an interview with Veronica Hermann at eleven a.m. They sat in her library, arrayed with bookcases, tea services, and overstuffed chairs. The intoxicating scent of Gardenias drifted through the open bay windows overlooking a gorgeously landscaped back yard.

"Thank you for agreeing to speak with us, Mrs. Hermann," O'Shea said.

"It surprised me when Major Davidson called to request this interview. It seemed odd that the fiancé of the second victim of my husband's murder wanted to speak with me. But I believe I understand, Mr. McNally, as we share the unthinkable misfortune of that day."

Kyle smiled ruefully, and said, "I am terribly sorry for your loss, Mrs. Hermann. I know it's difficult for you to speak about it so soon after his death. I've struggled with feelings about my own loss that day.

"My involvement in this investigation was approved by the Tampa Police Department, and we're trying to locate the killer before the trail goes cold. Since I'm certain my fiancée wasn't the assassin's target, I'm wondering how Mr. Hermann was."

He paused for a moment to give Veronica a chance to consider her response, watching for any sign of stress in her speech or body language.

"Mrs. Hermann, do you have any suspicions about who might have wanted your husband killed? Were there any issues you could share with us? Perhaps trouble at work? Or even, maybe, here at home?"

"At home? God no! Felix and I were a team. He shared everything with me, and I with him. He knew the stores where I shopped, where my girlfriends and I ate lunch, had my hair and nails done, and who I played golf with at the country club. He even knew my bank balances. And, I've got money of my own." She turned slightly away from Kyle, and mumbled, "A couple doesn't get much closer than that, does it?"

Kyle paused, jotting a couple quick notes before responding.

"No, I suppose not. Perhaps other possible complications? Did he share any issues at Black Dragon with you?"

"No. Nothing he told me beyond the usual office politics."

"Any suggestions of problems with his co-workers?"

"No, none."

"Any possible problems with gambling or drinking?"

"No. Felix bragged about his near-obsessive self-control. I sometimes poked fun at him about it."

"How about with any friends or family members? Was there anyone he mentioned having difficulty with?"

When tears welled in Mrs. Hermann's eyes, O'Shea intervened, "I know this is difficult ma'am, but we're hoping to learn if your husband was under unusual pressure; something that could point us to a potential suspect."

"Yes, I understand. But that doesn't make it any easier," she said, wringing her hands on her lap.

"You mentioned office politics, Mrs. Hermann. Could you talk more about that?" Kyle said.

"He told me about a conversation with Dom that occurred not long ago. Apparently, it concerned Scott Kaine, their lead software developer. He didn't get into specifics about it, just said Kaine's always been eccentric. And it was complicated because Dom insisted on hiring

Scott, even though early on, Felix opposed it. You know, they all served together in Iraq."

"Yes, Mr. Papadapolis shared that with me. Did your husband tell you why he objected to Mr. Kaine's hiring?"

"Not directly, but he suggested it was about something that happened in Iraq. He never told me what it was. However, over time, he came to respect Scott's work for the company."

"Thank you, Mrs. Hermann. Were there any other changes in your husband's circumstances that could be connected to this tragedy?"

Mrs. Hermann daubed her eyes, swallowed hard, and her shoulders fell.

"Take your time, ma'am," O'Shea said.

"Felix was preparing to leave Black Dragon. He'd already received two bona fide offers from other security companies. He was very excited about one."

"Did he discuss it with his partner, Mr. Papadapolis?" Kyle said.

"He didn't tell me."

"Thank you, Mrs. Hermann. Anything else you'd like to add?"

"No, Felix was well liked by everyone who knew him. He is…he… he was a personality plus person."

Kyle and O'Shea stood to leave. "Thank you for your cooperation, Mrs. Hermann."

WHEN THEY WERE back in the car, Kyle said, "There's something more there; something she didn't say."

"What do you mean?"

"I want to learn more about Scott Kaine and the trouble in Iraq she mentioned. And, though I certainly feel empathy for Mrs. Hermann, her husband sounded very controlling. I suspect it may have bothered her more than she lets on."

O'Shea's eyes brightened as she said, "Yes, the way she described their relationship as a team. I'd bet *his* description of their team would have been different from hers. And, it might not be a bad idea to find out if Mr. Hermann had a non-disclosure agreement with Black Dragon. If he did, it would complicate his options for leaving the partnership with Papadapolis."

Kyle liked O'Shea's instincts, saying, "Did you notice how several of her answers were spoken mechanically, without any feeling? I believe I'll need to visit Mrs. Hermann again soon."

CHAPTER 33

KYLE AND CORPORAL O'Shea sat down for lunch in the Guadalupe Room at Sagua La Grande. Tony joined them shortly after.

"Corporal Shannon O'Shea, this is my partner, Tony Petrocelli," Kyle said. "He's just joined me at the Paladin Detective Agency. We worked together as detectives in Chicago for several years before I moved down here."

"Nice to meet you, Tony. You can call me Shannon. Kyle has spoken very highly of you. Congratulations on your new position."

"Pleased to meet you, Shannon," Tony offered with an engaging smile.

"How'd your interview with Mrs. Hermann go this morning, Kyle?"

"We learned a couple of interesting things about her husband. Though I've gotta say, I was struck by her reserve in talking about a job offer he was pursuing. He planned to quit Black Dragon. That would likely create problems for his partner, Papadapolis.

"We also learned of a possible tie-in with their tech guy, Scott Kaine. Seems there was some friction within the administrative team that went beyond their Y2K problems.

"So, how'd your first day shadowing our new client go? Anything interesting?" Kyle asked.

"Nah. So far, no sign of anyone paying any unusual attention to her. She didn't have any plans to go out this afternoon, so I'm available for anything you need me to pick up."

"Tonight would be a good night to begin our reconnaissance of the Ybor parks. It's been five days since Y2K last struck. So far, all the murders have been pinned by forensics as falling between ten p.m. and midnight. That's our target range for surveillance."

"The last two murders occurred in Desoto and Cuscadan Parks, so he likes to move around. He's also increasing his pace. With these kinds of crimes, that implies he's becoming desperate. He believes the year 2000 is closing in on him and, face it, he'd be no good without his Y2K moniker." Then, smirking, said, "'Y2K+1' wouldn't compliment his demented poetic style.

"I'm told his first two murders also occurred in Ybor parks, though that was before the Trib received the first Haiku. Correct, Shannon?"

"Yes, Kyle. You've pointed out aspects which haven't been mentioned in our meetings, like Y2K's pace and motivation. As it turns out, I'm off tonight and tomorrow." Then, fixing her gaze directly at Tony, said, "Would it be too much to ask if I tagged along?"

Tony glanced at Kyle, hesitated for a second, then leaned in and said, "You'd be welcome to ride with me, Shannon."

Kyle directed a wry grin at Tony, and said, "So here's my plan: Why don't you two cover both Robles and Nebraska Avenue parks, and I'll watch the 18th Street and Highland Pines parks. Tony, if you need me, call my cell phone."

"It still surprises me that you own a cell phone," Tony said. And, to O'Shea, "Kyle's been a committed luddite since the day I met him."

Kyle tried futilely to affect a mocking frown. "Yeah, yeah, get over it fella."

LIEUTENANT WILLCOX AND Sergeant Dallas entered the cantina. As they were sitting, Willcox noticed Kyle, Tony, and Shannon seated together in the Guadalupe Room. He rose and walked to their table with a smirk stuck on his face.

He stopped abruptly behind Kyle, and glaring at O'Shea, said, "So, should I be surprised that you're joining the Paladin crew for a happy meal?"

Kyle turned slowly in his chair and, with eyes narrowed, pointed to an empty seat, and said, "Lieutenant Willcox, what a *nice* surprise. I'd ask you to join us, but as you can see, there are no *available* seats here."

O'Shea set down her fork and straightened in her chair before replying. "Nick, respectfully, Major Davidson asked me to accompany Mr. McNally to interview the wife of Felix Hermann, the man targeted on the fifth."

"You did? I wasn't notified. As a member of my team, you're required to advise me of all duty assignments you take, whether related to our case or not."

"You weren't at the station, but I signed out on the duty board. Didn't you notice? And I assumed the major would tell you as this is a follow-up to your interview."

"That's not routine," Willcox spat back.

Kyle clenched his fists as his head spun, glowering at Willcox. He'd listened to enough of that bullshit from his former commander in Chicago. His chair scraped loudly when he stood to face Willcox, who stood half a head shorter. He held up one hand saying, "Look Willcox, try to relax. The Corporal was ordered to re-interview Mrs. Hermann by your boss. She'll write up her report so you'll be made fully aware of any new information we learned. Now, how about you sit back down and enjoy your lunch. We'll finish ours, then the Corporal will get back to the station and submit her report."

As he turned to walk away, the Lieutenant said, "I'll speak more with you back at the station, O'Shea."

After Willcox was out of the room, Tony said, "Holy shit! First impressions, right? Now that I've met him, I swear to God, if I saw that guy drowning in Hillsborough Bay, I throw him an anchor."

Kyle grinned mischievously, and O'Shea shot an appreciative smile at Tony.

CHAPTER 34

WITH A SHAKY voice, the caller said, "Hello Dire."

"I trust you're on a burner phone."

"Of course. You get the fifty grand I wired you?"

"Yes. And, I don't need to remind you, this was a one-off. Your favor's repaid. We're done."

"Nice work."

"I know."

"No one around here has a clue who did it. But now there's a private eye involved. The boyfriend of the woman who went down with the target that day. He's working with the Tampa PD, but it's okay, they're stuck. I'd keep an eye out for him though."

"Gotta name for this bloke? I'll need you to tell me if he gets close. Who is he?"

"McNally. Kyle McNally. Operates the Paladin Detective Agency here in Ybor City. He appears to be competent."

"It'd take a bloody miracle to find me. *Do not* ring me again but for an emergency. And, I'll not remind you, if you ever wish to commit suicide, tell another soul about our arrangement. We're done. *Do you understand?*"

"Of course, I'm smarter than that."

CHAPTER 35

KYLE, PATRICK, AND Tony sat at a table at Finnegan's Wake Irish Pub on 8th Avenue waiting for their friend, Leo Davidson. Patrick was tapping a finger on the rim of his Teeling Blackpitts Irish Whiskey. Kyle took a deep drink of his usual Maker's Mark on the rocks. Tony stared bemusedly at his Captain Morgan Hurricane cocktail, served in a squall glass with half a day's worth of fruit sticking out of the top.

Patrick swirled his whiskey and, keenly taking the measure of Kyle, said, "Kyle m'lad, how're ya holdin' up these days? It's been a week since you laid dear Mykel to rest. Such a fine woman. No fate could've been crueler to the both of you."

Kyle took a big swallow of his drink and said, "Fate? This wasn't fate, Patrick. I'm numb from the neck up. It's like being slowly choked since her death. I keep circling back to the recognition that if I'd been five minutes earlier, I might've saved her."

"Hang on a moment son, there's no use swimmin' in that pool of regret. You're hurtin' right now, sure. But if you spend enough time there, they'll be fishin' you out at the end of a pole hook. You'll find a way back. I'm here with ya son."

"You had nothing to do with Mykel's death, Kyle," Tony said. "You didn't kick that hornet's nest. It was an indefensible accident initiated by another man's malevolent purpose."

"I don't give a shit, Tony. The score is one to nothing, and I'll be damned if I don't even it up."

The echoes of boisterous conversations, football score announcements on TV, and clinking glasses was interrupted when the pub patrons went silent and turned their heads in unison; Leo Davidson, a man nearly the size of biblical Goliath, entered through the front door. He walked up to their table and boomed, "Hey guys. What the hell? You starting without me?"

Patrick responded, "One drink? That's a far piece from gettin' started, my friend."

When all had a fresh round, Leo asked, "Patrick, any news from your Interpol contacts about our sniper?"

"Matter of fact, I've just come by updates concerning our shooter this morning from my former lad, Seamus Joyce. First, this is certainly the man I spoke about, 'Dire.' Their comparisons of rifle and caliber choice confirmed it.

"Second, they last had him moving to the U.S., somewhere in the southeast. That checks a box.

"Third, they're followin' up on leads concerning a Brit sniper and his short-term military TDY assignments. Name's Christopher Cross, and likely our *Dire*. Reports tell he trained in the sniper platoon of the Brit's First Fusiliers, Armored Infantry Battlegroup. It was normal for the Brits and the U.S. to share assets in Iraq, so they're checkin' for any ties between his British duty stations and U.S. military attachments."

Kyle's arm flew out, nearly knocking his drink off the table, "Fuck me! This guy's name is 'Chris Cross?'"

Leo jumped in. "That's good news Patrick. At least now we've got a name."

"Kyle, that's what you tried to tell me when we worked together in Chicago," Tony said. "There are some people, like the Slugger, and this Chris Cross, who have a latent ability to live without conscience."

Kyle flashed a lopsided smile, and replied, "I don't recall saying that *exactly*, Tony." After their subdued chuckles subsided, all raised their glass in commitment to Mykel's memory and downed their drinks.

CHAPTER 36

KYLE STRODE INTO the offices of Black Dragon Security Solutions. The receptionist greeted him, "Hello again Mr. McNally. Mr. Papadapolis is expecting you."

Dom stepped out of his office and said, "Please come in, Kyle."

When they were seated, Dom asked, "What exactly did you call about, Kyle? Your call was unexpected."

"Actually Dom, it's about my conversation with Mrs. Hermann, your partner's widow."

Dominic stiffened, and said, "Well, I'm certain I can't be of any help to you there."

"I only have a couple of questions. The first is about Felix. She told me he was planning to leave your company."

Bristling, he said, "She told you that?"

"Yes."

"My second concerns some personnel issues here at Black Dragon."

"How exactly does that relate to your case with my wife?" he said, studying Kyle.

"Not directly. But I am working with TPD on my fiancée's murder, and have their authorization to follow leads related to the assassin's intended target, your partner Felix Hermann."

"I've already answered questions from the police concerning what I know, and didn't know, about any threats to Felix. I'll talk about what little I know, but you'll be disappointed. Yes, Felix and I talked about his possible leaving, and the offers he'd gotten. He was too valuable to let him go without proposing a counter offer. I made him a generous one. He told me he'd consider it. He was a one-of-a-kind in our business. And, of course, he was my close personal friend."

"Was your offer put on paper?"

Dom shrugged. "Well, no, it was only a verbal discussion at that point. I had to involve my lawyers on any contract revisions. This just came up the week before his death."

"That's reasonable; and I suspect your lawyers may be able to verify any conversations concerning a contract revision for Felix."

"To be honest, we'd been so busy around here with travel, and the Y2K problems, I hadn't found time to follow-up. Felix knew I was working on it for him though. If you're unfamiliar with lawyer's procedures, they can take weeks to produce contract documentation."

"But there were notes, right?"

Papadapolis leaned back in his chair, crossing his arms. "Mr. McNally, you've got me curious." He tilted his head and continued, "Why is any of this of interest to you? There's no obvious relationship with either my wife's case you're handling, or to the apprehension of Mr. Hermann's murderer. This case falls under the jurisdiction of the Tampa PD. Am I missing something here?" he said, with a shake of his head.

Glancing down at his notepad, Kyle took a moment before answering. "No, Dom. But to answer you, I'm trying to resolve questions from my interview with Mrs. Hermann. She mentioned learning from her husband about ongoing friction here at Black Dragon. Did I misunderstand her? I know people sometimes don't recall facts accurately."

"As for that, well yes, there's been some tension around here concerning the Y2K problems. Tempers flared between Scott and Felix, but I didn't believe it was anything more than a little dustup. Felix was unhappy with the pace of Scott's work on the fixes." He straightened slightly, and asked, "Why? Is it your idea that either of them could have escalated the disagreement?"

Kyle leaned in and said, "Perhaps, but if you don't mind, I'd like a chance to talk with Mr. Kaine about it. I'm certain he'll confirm what you've told me. Would you arrange it? I'd like to resolve any potential links to my fiancée's, and your partner's, murder."

Dominic gave a half shrug and said, "I don't see the harm in that, though I can't imagine there's any connection." He called Kaine and told him Kyle would stop by to speak with him.

"Thank you, Dom."

Standing to leave, Kyle stopped and asked, "Oh, and one more thing Dom, did Felix have a non-disclosure agreement with Black Dragon?"

"No, we never felt the need for one. More of a gentleman's agreement."

KYLE APPROACHED THE receptionist and asked to be directed to Mr. Kaine's office. Rising, she said, "Please follow me," and led him to an office several doors down the hall. She tapped on the door. Kaine was talking on the phone, waving Kyle in.

Kaine didn't rise when Kyle entered. He still had the goatee and hipster mustache, but without the costumed outfit. Placing his hand over the microphone, he said, "Hello. Dom told me you were coming by. Take a load off," nodding to a chair.

He had a fair complexion, but appeared to be on the wrong side of anorexia. Dozens of mythical creatures from the popular *Dungeons and Dragons* games decorated his office, and a snowstorm of post-it notes blanketed almost every vertical surface. He replaced the phone on its cradle and said, "Dom didn't tell me the reason you wanted to talk with me. Kinda creepy with what's been going on around here lately."

"Hello, Mr. Kaine. Nice to meet you. May I ask what exactly you mean when you say 'what's been going on around here lately'?" Kyle took out his notepad and pencil.

"Well, since Felix's murder, the rumors have been swirling. Cops have been here several times and Dom's been out of the office a lot. There's a whole different vibe around this place, is all."

Kyle shook his head and said, "Are you talking about some of the problems between you and Mr. Hermann?" He sat back in his chair and scratched a quick notation.

Kaine tugged and twirled at the right side of his mustache. "Yeah, sure, there had been some differences between us, but I respected Mr. H. Why're you asking? Did Dom say anything about it to you? Ya know, before he hired me, we served together in Iraq. Ever since, he's been like a big brother to me."

"Of course. That's only natural. I'm interested in learning more about it. Tell me about your time with Dom and Felix in the military. Where, and how exactly did you meet?"

"We were stationed together at FOB Cobra, just outside of Baghdad. Dom was a Lieutenant Colonel and our battalion commander. Felix was a captain, one of Dom's three company commanders. I met Dom when I was a Second Lieutenant, fresh out of Officer Candidate School. I worked as a staff officer and studied computer programming at a correspondent school. Driving for Dom, I got to know them both."

"Thank you for your service, Mr. Kaine. I spoke with Mrs. Hermann yesterday and she mentioned she'd heard about some friction between you and her husband. Could you tell me more?"

Kaine tugged at his mustache again. "She did? I wonder how she heard that. It's too bad for her. Real bad. You see, Felix and I normally got along good. But ever since this Year 2000 scare got legs, he went over-the-top, acting paranoid about my ability to get it taken care of. He complained about me to Dom and I gotta say, honestly, that pissed me off. Talk about disrespect. He never did that before."

After jotting a quick note, Kyle continued. "And, was it 'taken care of?'"

"Well, I'm ninety-five percent there, now that Mr. P and Mr. H brought the hammer down on our overseas clients. So yes, we'll be in compliance by January one. I had that wrapped days before he was killed. He was relieved; even thanked me."

"Certainly, but with all that, did your problems ever go beyond arguing? I'd understand, if I was in your shoes."

"Nah, it never boiled over. At least, not for me."

"Mrs. Hermann told me something else. She said you were arrested while serving there. She thought it was something pretty bad, maybe enough to get you discharged. Felix told her about it. What was it about?"

He shot bolt upright and looked down, saying, "Really? She told you that?"

"Yes."

"Well, it wasn't anything like that."

"What was it *like*?"

"It was a stupid misunderstanding…wrong place, wrong time. I was off base and arrested for a crime I didn't commit. The local scumbag cops were out to get us GIs. I guess we were their prime targets for promotions. Dom helped me out of it."

"How did he do it?"

"I never asked him, and he never offered. But two days later, I was back on the base."

"I see. Dom also mentioned to me you and your longtime girlfriend recently split. Sorry to hear that."

"He did? I'm surprised. We didn't talk much about it, but yeah, me and my old lady did break-up a couple months back. She cracked up on me. I'd finally had enough, so I kicked her out of my place. Good riddance, I say."

"Would it be okay if I spoke with her, Mr. Kaine? Dom didn't believe it would be a problem," Kyle bluffed.

Kaine shifted in his seat. "He did, really? Well then, I guess it'd be okay. Just so you know, she'll probably chew heavily on me because of my breakup with her. We'd been together since high school."

"Don't worry about that. Your relationship with her isn't my concern.

Standing to leave, Kyle raised a finger and asked, "Oh, by the way, Mr. Kaine, did you earn your sharpshooter badge when you were in the army?"

"Nah, I only got the simple one in basic training. Never really warmed up to rifles."

Kyle thanked Kaine and left with Joyce McKensey's address and phone number.

CHAPTER 37

B Y TEN O'CLOCK, Kyle and Patrick were eating breakfast at the Sagua La Grande. Rosa had just refilled their coffee cups when Guillermo walked over to their table and gave Kyle's shoulder a squeeze.

"Any news of the man who murder Mykel?"

"No."

Throwing his arms up, Guillermo burst out, "Cabrón! Enterraré al hombre profundamente en el suelo!"

"Huh?" Patrick said.

Rosa scowled at Guillermo before responding. "He says the man is a bastard, and he will bury him deep in the ground when he is found."

"I'm sorry to you Rosa, and you gentlemen; sometime, my anger is too hot."

Kyle shook his head and gave a reassuring nod to Rosa before speaking. "No need to apologize. Like you, I won't be satisfied until we catch him.

"But I know Mykel wasn't his target, so I've begun investigating the background of the man who was shot with her.

"And, now that Tony has joined the agency, we're working together on your friend Queasy's murder. While the Tampa police have increased their surveillance of the Ybor parks, Tony and I are taking shifts as well."

Guillermo briefly crossed himself before replying, "I am happy to hear this. The people in Ybor fear the crazy man who kill us in our city."

CHAPTER 38

THE CLOUDS WERE inky black on a late, blustery Thursday afternoon in Tampa when Leo entered the offices of Paladin Detective Agency. Kyle was compiling notes on the Y2K case.

"Whoo boy! That wind's been trying to blow my ass to Bradenton on the way over here," Leo said, unbuttoning his uniform jacket. "Catch you at a good time, Kyle?"

"Yeah, come on in Leo. I'm collecting my notes for you on Y2K. You want coffee? Or, I was just about to crack a bottle of Maker's Mark if you'd prefer something a little more therapeutic."

"Been a rough day. I'll take a couple fingers, thanks."

Relaxed and seated with their feet up, the two men enjoyed a few moments of quiet peace while sipping their drinks. With a tight smile and a shake of his head, Leo spoke first, "Willcox and my team haven't made a Goddamn bit of progress on our investigation. No updates from forensics on the footprints found at Cuscadan Park. And nothing yet on the database search for the three letter initials. What the hell? Please tell me you found something new."

"I've come across one sketchy lead, but I'm far from certain about it. I'll share it with you as soon as I get answers to a couple more questions."

"Anything you need help with?"

"No. Not yet. At this point, my information is coming from pretty far out in left field."

"Don't hold back too long Kyle; pressure from above is getting heavy."

"I get that. I'm still waiting to hear back from your lab on the identification of the car badge, and the photos and paint scraping I gave them. Could you follow up on that for me?"

"I will. Has Patrick learned anything more from his Interpol friends about our sniper, Dire?"

Kyle shrugged his shoulders. "Nothing new. He tells me they've been slow responding to his inquiries."

KYLE WAS ABOUT to head home when his phone rang.

"Kyle. Good. I'm glad I caught you in. I must see you!"

"Something wrong, Jo?"

"Dominic's out of town again on *business,* he says. Now my daily charts are pointing to a catastrophic event on the near horizon. Dangerous tides are rising around me Kyle."

"I'm sorry Jo. Tony's still shadowing you, right?"

"Yes, but I know someone's after me. Can you *please* help me."

"Not today, Jo, but I'll stop by your place first thing in the morning?"

"Sure…I just hope it won't be too late."

CHAPTER 39

KYLE ARRIVED AT Jolene Papadapolis' Bayshore Drive residence at 8:30 a.m. He knocked on the door, and it opened almost immediately. Her posture was tense, and her Barbie pajamas were twisted around her body. Just before she closed the door, a chilling gust of wind carried the hint of an early morning rain. She held an iced cocktail in one hand.

"Where have you been? Come in quickly. I don't want my snoopy neighbors seeing me."

"I'm here now, Jo. What's got you concerned. Have you received any threats?"

She slapped a hand on the door frame, and her lips tightened into an impatient scowl. "Concerned? Am I concerned?" she snapped. "Do I look concerned? Last night, there was a man crossing my property, just in back of my sea nymph," she said, waving wildly at her backyard.

"Your sea nymph?"

"My mermaid fountain; my good luck talisman. But tell me, am I going to need 24-hour protection to get any peace of mind in my own home? I didn't get a second's sleep last night."

"Tell me more. When you saw him, did he acknowledge or threaten you in any way?"

Jo stomped her foot and blurted, "No, but he was on my property! Doesn't that mean anything to you?" *Why doesn't he understand?*

"Just a minute Jo. I promise you; your safety and security are my highest priorities. Tony's been in close contact, hasn't he?"

"Sure—sure he has. But that's cold comfort for me. I'm here all alone while my husband's out somewhere doin' God knows what. I've got a pretty good notion he's been getting together with the newly-minted widow Hermann." *Does he think I'm crazy?*

"This is the first time you've mentioned her name in connection with Dominic. Have you asked him about her?"

"No. But that woman always played possum around me. I never trusted her," Jo said, shaking her head and wagging a finger at him. "She was always checkin' him out; her doe eyes didn't fool me. No sir, not even a little." *That little snake!*

"When will your husband be home?"

"He was supposed to call me and tell me; but nothing for two nights now, so I'm not sure."

"So, are you worried about him?"

"Worried about him? Hell no! He's a grown-ass man," she said, with trembling hands and bright, flushed cheeks.

"Jo, if you honestly believe you need more protection, I'll schedule it with Tony, for you. I spoke with him earlier; he says he's seen no suspicious activity around either you or your home in the week and a half he's tailed you."

Her shoulders slumped, and she turned away. "Nah, I guess not just yet. But please, *please* don't forget about me." *You're my last hope, Kyle!*

"That'll never happen Jo."

Kyle walked to his car under a darkening sky with gusting, wind-driven rain falling.

CHAPTER 40

TWO HOURS LATER, Kyle and Tony were having lunch together at Sagua La Grande. The meal was interrupted by the sudden crashing of glasses, cups, saucers, and silverware dumped from a tray, to the complete embarrassment of a young busboy. Heightening his shame, several of the patrons good-naturedly cheered and applauded his calamity. Rosalina quickly jumped in to lend comfort and help to the crest-fallen youth.

After clearing and cleaning the mess, Rosa raised both hands splayed out over her tilted head and offered a public apology, which garnered applause and approval from the guests.

"Tony, Jo's at her wit's end. I'm afraid she could be on the verge of a nervous breakdown. I hope I'm wrong, but when I met with her earlier, I saw someone who's coming unraveled."

"What did she say? Did she say anything about me?"

"Not about you. Her latest rant started with a phone call last night. I met with her this morning and she was frazzled. She'd seen a trespasser on the back of her property, but I don't believe she was in any danger. She was acting more fidgety than a chihuahua in an elephant pen."

"Sorry, Kyle. Do you believe she needs additional coverage? I mean, that's one thing we could offer her."

"I asked, but she declined. Let's keep a close eye on her. Try checking in with her more often when you're on duty. I will also speak with her husband again when he's back in town. I've got questions for him about his relationship with Mrs. Hermann, one that Jo alluded to."

"Will do, Kyle," Tony said. "Oh, and I wanted to remind you that Shannon will be joining me tonight for the park surveillance."

With emphasis on her rank and surname, Kyle said, "By Shannon, I'm assuming you mean Corporal O'Shea, right?"

"Well, yeah. We've been getting along pretty well. Even been out on a couple of dates."

He smiled and said, "I'm happy for you. She's a nice young lady and a promising policewoman. I also believe she'll make a good detective."

Guillermo approached their table and said, "Gentlemen, how were your meals? May I have Rosa bring you more coffee?"

"No, thank you Guillermo," Kyle said. "So you know, I spoke with Leo last night, and he tells me his detectives haven't learned anything new about the identity of Y2K. Have you heard anything more about suspicious men in the parks lately around your neighborhoods?"

"Now you mention it, I did speak with a man earlier I wished to tell to you about. He call himself Mr. Atlas; un poco loco. But he say a man came by once, but is different now."

"Different how?" Kyle said.

"He tell me this man drive by his casa more now."

"Any idea where Mr. Atlas lives?"

"He sleep at a left house across from the park on 18th Avenue."

"Left house?" Kyle asked, "Do you mean an abandoned house?"

"Sí."

"Do you know where he is, Guillermo?" Tony said.

"I do. He sit in my alley now."

"We'd like to speak with Mr. Atlas. Could you introduce us, Guillermo?" Kyle said. "I don't want to scare him. He may be more comfortable with you there."

"Sí. Anything that help to find this ghost that kill mi amigo."

They approached Atlas in the alley behind the cantina. He sat on an overturned trash can. Deep creases in his face and a ruddy, bulbous nose surrounded two squinty blue eyes. Shocks of unkempt salt and pepper hair straggled out from beneath a beat-up herringbone newsboy cap.

"Mr. Atlas, these are mis amigos, Kyle and Tony."

"Gentlemen, it's an honor to meet you," Atlas said in a theatrically booming voice and a flourish of his rumpled cap.

"Pleased to meet you, Mr. Atlas," Kyle said. "That's an interesting surname. I'm curious, is Atlas your given name?"

"How interesting of you to inquire about it, Mr. Kyle. Actually, I was festooned by my colleagues with that moniker during my youthful years in academia. It seems they believed I was blessed with a rather deity-like aptitude for professorial endeavors," he said, again loudly, with his chin rising and a twinkle in his eyes.

"Quite the honor. Guillermo tells me you may have noticed a stranger cruising in your neighborhood recently. Is that true?"

"Indubitably."

"Could you identify the driver?"

"Well, in truth, he was but a silhouette inside his vehicle, which I'm certain was cerulean in color."

"You mean dark blue?" Tony asked.

"Yes, of course," Atlas said, in a condescending tone of voice.

"So you couldn't identify the driver?" Kyle said.

"Nay, as I say, the driver was a mere shade."

"Any other noteworthy observations or details you might share with us?" Kyle said.

"The several times I witnessed this knavish character hovering; it was always within an hour or two following sundown. Might that be of any help?"

"Yes, in fact it is."

While Kyle scratched a couple of quick notes, Tony stood and said, "Thank you very much, Mr. Atlas. It may be your suspicious driver is the very knave we seek now. Please provide us with the location of your current domicile. We'd love to confabulate further, however, at this time, your full name and address would be most assistive."

"Mr. Tony, I am exhilarated by your obvious flair for the King's English. Of course, I am obliged to provide you with my current residence's locale," Atlas boomed with a tilt of his head. Then, after swatting away some interested flies, he meticulously replaced and readjusted the filthy cap on his head.

When they'd returned to the car, Kyle said, "I'll bet that Mr. Atlas has lived his entire life at the top of his voice. And Tony, that was quite a demonstration of the King's English back there. Cerulean? Domicile? Confabulate? Sometimes you still surprise me."

"Good," Tony said. Then, with a broad grin and the tip of an imaginary cap, "I've been waiting to use those words for more than a year now."

"Following up on Mr. Atlas' information, I'm gonna take a few turns around East Ybor and 18th Avenue Parks tonight. Might get lucky. Why don't you and Corporal O'Shea monitor the Tampa Park Plaza area," Kyle said, pulling out onto Fifth Avenue, heading back to their offices.

CHAPTER 41

KYLE KNOCKED ON the door of Joyce McKensey's apartment. The woman answering was a disheveled, four foot nine-inch Latino lady in a sheer blouse that struggled to contain her ample, braless breasts. She sported Jamaican dreadlocks, a shaved right eyebrow, and tattoo sleeves running down both arms while looking him up and down.

"Yeah, wha'dya want."

"Hello, Miss McKensey? I'm Kyle McNally," he said, handing her his card. "I called earlier about coming by to speak with you."

"Oh, sure. Would'na guessed you'd look like this though," she said, giving him the twice-over.

"May I come in?"

Kyle almost tripped over the stack of books under the corner of a dirty, broken love seat she directed him to. Her place was what might generously be called a studio apartment, and heavy with the mingled fragrances of patchouli incense and burnt chili peppers.

"Thank you for agreeing to speak with me. I'm here to ask about your former boyfriend, Scott Kaine. He mentioned that you'd broken up, but said you'd be okay with my visit."

"Kaine? That jerk? He turned out to be just a long lastin' boil on my ass. Yeah, we had a relationship, if you wanna call ten wasted years *that*. We fought, bit, kicked, and spit at each other for a time. Then he got too fuckin' weird."

"How do you mean, too weird?"

Joyce's eyes widened. "What, you don't know weird? Yeah right, you're a private dick and you never seen weird?" she said with a snort. "I tell ya, Scott got weird. Started spoutin' off mumbo jumbo, callin' himself the next comin' of Henry David Whitman, or somethin' like that. Never mind his PTSD shit I had to put up with."

"He wrote poetry?"

"Yeah, sure, if that's what you'd call it. Me, I never got it. So anyway, between that and his obsession with that stupid-ass computer game, Dingleberries and Dragons, I'd had enough. He even made me start callin' him by his first name, Axel, after he fell in love with Guns and Roses' music. You believe that shit? Even when everyone else still called him Scott. So yeah, that was his kinda weird.

"And those stupid stories about his mom he *loved* to tell. You'da gotten the idea she was his prison cell mate."

Kyle scratched a couple of quick notes and asked, "Stories?"

"Yeah. He kept yappin' about the stupid shit she used to say, like, 'You're the only hell I ever raised.' I expect it made him feel more like a man. Always got him hard though, so I didn't mind that.

"Oh, and how about the clown suit getup he liked to wear? He'd dress up like the Sultan of Sanibel and head downtown for God knows what reasons. You'da believed he was smokin' crack, right?"

"I saw him wearing that outfit," Kyle said as he rose to leave. "Thank you, Miss McKensey. I appreciate your speaking with me. I'll let myself out."

"You sure you wouldn't like to stay for a drink, or maybe somethin' else?" she asked with a suggestive smile.

"No, but thanks anyway."

"Ya know, I always said that a 'no' is just a 'yes' dressed up in a raincoat. You sure?" she said, with one hand tugging at the top button of her too tight blouse.

Kyle was half way to the door when he turned, smiled, and said, "Thanks again Joyce."

Your fear grows with each new dawn.
Trust me, I won't stop!
I'm the avenger you wrought.
Don't guess who I am, just ask.

\- Y2K

CHAPTER 42

I **SPOT MY** prey sitting on a bench underneath a live oak tree's mossy tentacles. I am at my third Ybor park of the night having had no luck previously. It's a cool, overcast night with a sliver moon peeking in and out between broken clouds. I settle my car into a spot on the dead end of 22nd Avenue, facing the railroad tracks. I step out into the shiver-inducing night air. I'm struck by a strong odor of locomotive diesel fuel competing with a strange, but compelling sense of dusky dread rapping on the back door of my mind.

He's a vagrant asleep on a park bench. I creep toward him from behind. Now, standing over him, I spend a moment savoring my own rising exhilaration. I take a swipe at the drool from my lips, greedily anticipating the grace I'm about to bestow on this poor unconscious fool. *He earned this. The people sentenced him. I'm here to execute a judgement the world finds him guilty of…uselessness!*

I gently tap him on the shoulder. "Pardon me."

He jumps from the bench and turns to face me. His sagging, sodden face frozen behind immense, terrified eyes. "N-no. Who are you?"

"You don't know me, but I'm about to become your best friend," I say as I reach into my left jacket pocket and produce a pint of rot gut vodka. I walk around the bench smiling, extending the bottle out to him in a friendly gesture.

"L-look meester, why don' you go a-way. I don' wan' no booze. Just leaves me 'lone, hokay?"

"Well, then maybe a couple of the candy bars I brought," I say, reaching into my right-hand pocket, grabbing my switchblade by the hilt, whipping it out, and activating the blade release. The poor slob hears the sudden metallic click-click, and his eyes fly wide open as his mouth twists in horror. My first blow comes from the right, severing his trachea, followed by a second swipe, a backhanded strike from the left, opening his right carotid artery, completing my ritual technique.

He collapses back onto the bench, grasping his neck with both hands, making final, frantic gestures at deliverance. And tonight, his hopelessly wasted life ends with no fanfare.

I stand back to admire the pulse-driven ruby surges of blood, a glorious testament to my success. It pleases me.

Then there was the scrape of a shoe heel on the pavement behind me.

CHAPTER 43

WITH ONLY THE intermittent pale light of a crescent moon to guide him, Kyle could barely make out the two men near a bench as he cruised the 18th Street Park. He stopped, exited the vehicle, and cautiously approached. One man was seated and the other stood in front of him. Drawing closer, Kyle realized the man on the bench was slouched over, unmoving.

"Hey mister, is there a problem here?" Kyle said, positioning his right hand for quick access to the Sig Sauer in his shoulder holster.

The man turned slightly left, revealing his profile. Kyle thought he recognized him…*Could it be?*

The man hesitated for a moment before replying, "Trouble? No trouble here," still concealing his right hand. "I noticed this poor guy here, and I stopped to check on him."

Kyle noted the man's balled left fist and clenched jaw; it was time to escalate the contact. "Okay buddy, I need you to turn and face me with both hands over your head."

From where the suspect stood, he blocked Kyle's view of the seated man. Kyle took a quick step to the right and realized the seated man was covered in blood from neck to knees. It still trickled from two long gashes on his neck.

Just as Kyle pulled his pistol from its holster, the suspect spun rapidly, whipping his right arm directly at Kyle. With a loud, metallic click-click and a flash of silver in the man's hand, Kyle dodged backward, too late to avoid the attacker's swipe at him. It slashed him on his defensively raised left arm. Completing his swing, the hilt of the assailant's knife knocked the gun from Kyle's outstretched arm, where it clattered to the pavement.

Quickly recovering, Kyle knelt for one second before responding with a vicious right uppercut that caught the man directly in the groin. His attacker doubled over, expelling a wounded howl, ending with his head in close range of Kyle's next blow from the left to the temple. Kyle felt something crack in his left fist. *Damn!*

The force of Kyle's rapid second strike knocked the suspect off his feet. He sprawled on his back, blinking wildly, struggling for air. A second later, he sprang back to his feet and ran. Kyle chased, caught, and attempted to wrap his arms around the man to restrain him. The man began writhing madly, screaming, "Get your fuckin' hands off me!"

He spun again, now face to face with Kyle, and stabbed his switchblade into Kyle's left side below the rib cage. Eyes ablaze, Kyle roared and knocked the blade from the man's hand, before stumbling, and crumbled to his knees.

The suspect made a mad scramble and was gone before Kyle could react. He clutched the wound on his side with one hand and pressed Tony's speed dial on his cell phone with the other. Gasping for air, he said, "Tony, I'm at the 18th Street Park. I need help. Call for an ambulance, the perp nicked me with his knife. And notify TPD there's been another Y2K murder. He got away, but I've got evidence now."

CHAPTER 44

THEY KEPT KYLE at Tampa General overnight. When Patrick, Tony, and O'Shea stepped into his room at ten the next morning, Kyle sat on the bed with his hospital gown wrapped around his waist and no shirt on.

Eyeing Kyle's gauze-wrapped chest, carefully dressed left hand and right arm, Patrick said, "Well good, you look to be only a wee bit worse for the wear."

With a grimace, Kyle said, "I'll gladly trade my worse for yours, Patrick."

"Good to see you vertical this morning," Tony said, eyeing Kyle's clumsy moves to clamor down from his bed. "We brought your car, but if you'd rather not drive, Shannon—*then nervously,* I mean Corporal O'Shea—offered to take yours home for you."

"Thanks, but no thanks." Then wiggling the fingertips of his left hand, "I'm good to go Tony. And, save the *Corporal O'Shea* stuff for when you're with the TPD team, okay?" Glancing down at a bag Patrick held, he asked, "Is that my change of clothes?"

"Yes, son."

O'Shea spoke up. "Are you sure you shouldn't be staying here for the day, Kyle?" Then, turning away and screwing her face up in mock-horror at Tony, she continued, "I'm sorry, but with all that gauze wrapped around you, my guess is, you've been prepped for mummification."

With a half-hearted grin, Kyle said, "Yeah, very funny, O'Shea. But no, right now I need to bring the team up to speed on the Y2K killer. Crime scene had the switchblade tagged and bagged before the ambulance hauled me away. Any word yet, on a fingerprint ID?"

"Not before I left the station."

Kyle took the bag from Patrick and went to the bathroom to dress. When he returned, he said, "I'm sure I recognized the guy, but I'll wait for confirmation from forensics. So, how about you three get me out of this upscale nursing home now."

Patrick sat Kyle into the waiting wheelchair and pushed him down to his car in the parking lot. "Word of advice, son. You'd best be advised to go home for a day or two, Kyle."

"You're right. But I need to wrap this case, and my best bet is to do it today, if we're gonna catch Y2K before he runs."

WHEN LEO GREETED Kyle in the conference room at TPD, he moved in for a bear hug, but Kyle winced, holding him at arm's length, saying, "Not just yet major. I'm still pretty sore."

"You have no idea how good it is to *see you* again. Come on in and join us," motioning to Willcox, Dallas, and O'Shea.

"Any news from forensics on fingerprints yet?" Kyle asked.

"Not yet, but they should have a match soon," Willcox said. "That was a helluva risk you took last night McNally. I wish you'd notified the department about your plans yesterday."

Flashing a sardonic smile, Kyle said, "Yeah, sorry. I can't believe I forgot to do that, lieutenant. I assure you I won't forget next time,"

"So, Kyle, tell us about Y2K?" Major Davidson asked.

"He's five-foot eleven, with dark hair, medium build, dark blue eyes, a hipster mustache and goatee, and has one testicle lodged somewhere up in his abdomen. Oh, and I ID'd him."

"You what!" Dallas said.

Leo reached over and put his hand gently on Kyle's right arm. "You want to explain that, Kyle?"

"Sure. When he leapt at me with his knife, I recognized his face. I'd seen it before when I was interviewing him."

"Interviewing him?" O'Shea said.

"Yes, I first met him when I visited the Black Dragon Security Solutions offices. He's their lead programmer and security officer."

With a sly smirk, Willcox said, "Gotta name for us McNally?"

A knock on the door interrupted the meeting. An officer stepped in and said, "We've got an ID, major."

"Who is it, officer?"

"A Mr. Axel Scott Kaine, currently employed by Black Dragon Security Solutions Company, sir." She walked over to him and handed him the printout.

With a loud scrape from his chair, Lt. Willcox stood to leave the room.

"A-S-K," Major Davidson said.

CHAPTER 45

AFTER A MUCH-NEEDED day's rest, Kyle picked up Tony and drove to Jolene's home. "Tony, I want to make it clear to Jo we've seen no signs of either stalking or personal jeopardy over the past two weeks."

"You know how are you going to handle it?"

"Wish I knew. Right now, her fears are stuck a long way out front of anything provable. I've asked Leo about arranging for heightened police surveillance. But I don't believe that'll reassure her. I'll also talk again with Dominic, though I'm not convinced he'll be much help."

"HELLO, JO. WE'RE here today to call an end to your shadowing service." Her shoulders drooped and her chin fell to her chest. "Tony's been tracking you now for almost two weeks. And with no sign of anyone following or threatening you, I can't defend taking more of your money."

Shaking hands went to her face as she said, "I saw this coming Kyle. My recent charts are becoming more ominous. There are inferences pointing to the Ides of March, but I suspect the danger is much closer." *You…*

"I'm sorry. I wish I knew some way to reassure you."

She began shaking her head. "Honestly, Kyle, I'm not surprised. My assailants have gotten sneakier since Tony began trailing me." *…Just…*

"I spoke to my friend at the police department requesting more frequent drive-by coverage, so there'll be an officer nearby if you are threatened. I'll notify Dominic. And, of course, you can always call me or Tony in an emergency."

"Thanks, but that'll probably be too late." With tears in her eyes, and a sorrowful glance at Tony, Jolene walked over to Kyle and embraced him with a tender hug…*Don't Understand!*

Kyle and Tony drove back to Paladin Detective Agency without saying a word.

CHAPTER 46

KYLE RETURNED WITH Corporal O'Shea for a second interview with Veronica Hermann. He appreciated the comforting effect she had with the widow at their first interview.

He was looking for more information about the now missing Scott Kaine and her relationship with Dominic Papadapolis. He'd become suspicious of the coincidences surrounding the cabal of former army buddies at Black Dragon; one shot dead, and one, a serial killer, gone missing. He hoped she could provide some answers.

"Good morning, Mrs. Hermann. I'm sure you remember Corporal O'Shea," Kyle said.

"Thank you for agreeing to meet with us Mrs. Hermann. I know you're having to deal with many problems. Your grief must be immense," O'Shea said.

"I appreciate that, corporal. It's been difficult…to say the least."

Kyle said, "Unfortunately, Mrs. Hermann, there are problems in two of my cases that I hope you'll be able to help me with. The first one concerns Scott Kaine. After nearly capturing him in a murderous act three days ago, I'm seeking his whereabouts.

"The last time we spoke, you suggested there was trouble concerning him when he was serving with your husband in Iraq. I now believe it could help us discover where he may have gone. Anything specific about the trouble he got into over there? Maybe something your husband mentioned, or wrote to you about it?"

"In the three weeks since Felix was murdered, I've been going through the letters from him when he was in Iraq. I did come across one where he mentioned Scott. He said Kaine had gotten into some serious trouble. Something about civilian murders; something he said could get him court-martialed."

"Did your husband mention the charges?"

"Not specifically. But he thought they were serious enough to get Kaine discharged from the military; possibly even imprisoned. He also wrote that the charges were eventually dropped, implying it might have been engineered by Dominic."

"Mrs. Hermann, could you please share that letter with us? It may help locate Kaine," said Corporal O'Shea.

"Of course."

Throwing out bait, Kyle said, "Mrs. Hermann, the last time we spoke, did you mention you and your husband were having some difficulty in your marriage?"

"I said *that*? I don't recall. But I do remember we talked about troubles at Black Dragon."

Kyle took another step in. "The reason I'm reminded of it is that in speaking with Mrs. Papadapolis, she mentioned a suspicion that you may have been involved with her husband. Any idea where she got that idea?"

Veronica blinked, her head jerked back, and her mouth flew open. "What! She said that? What did she say?"

Neither Kyle nor O'Shea spoke for several seconds before Kyle said, "Is it possible that she may have been right?"

"Well, no," Veronica said. "You know, she's been sick a lot the past couple months. Dominic and I were good friends. He said our conversations were a comfort to him; mostly we talked about how difficult it was, living with her illnesses."

"But, were her suspicions about you and Dominic, correct?" Kyle said.

Her shoulders fell and her head bowed slightly before she spoke. "Yes…it shames me to admit her suspicions were correct."

"Mrs. Hermann, are you in love with Dominic Papadapolis?" O'Shea said.

"No. Absolutely not."

"Well then, had he'd fallen in love with you?"

"Looking back, I suppose so," Veronica said, now absent-mindedly raking her hands over her thighs.

"Did your relationship also involve physical intimacy?" O'Shea asked.

"Yes. I suppose I knew Dominic was falling in love with me. And I suppose I was genuinely flattered. He's a remarkably charismatic man. But I swear, I always made it clear to him that our relationship could never be serious. I love…I loved Felix. I never wished to harm him, and I'll live with that shame for the rest of my life. Our affair ended in late September."

Kyle leaned in and asked softly, "So Mrs. Hermann, isn't it just possible Dominic may have wanted your husband out of the picture? Out of *his* way?"

Veronica shifted uneasily in her seat before answering. "I don't think I like what you're implying, Mr. McNally. Is it your suggestion that I had anything to do with Felix's death. Or, that I could have prevented it?" She directed a pleading glance at O'Shea.

O'Shea said, "No, that's not what Mr. McNally is suggesting."

"Not at all, Mrs. Hermann. Forgive me, but I'm seeking clues about your husband's murder. I'm convinced his killing wasn't random, which leads me to conclude that someone who knew him may have been involved," Kyle said.

Recognizing her rising ire, O'Shea said, "Mrs. Hermann, I know how upsetting this is for you, but we've got to be certain we don't overlook any possibilities. Detective McNally isn't accusing you of any direct involvement in your husband's murder."

Mrs. Hermann bolted from her chair and paced to the bay windows overlooking her property. Arms crossed, and with her back to the two of them, she said, "Well, I should hope not."

"But isn't it remotely possible that Mr. Papadapolis could have been involved?" Kyle said.

Hot coals in her eyes, Veronica turned to them and barked, "No! And, this conversation is over. I demand you both leave now."

CHAPTER 47

BY THE TIME he got home, Kyle was exhausted and felt a stinging pain from his still-healing side wound. He pushed himself too hard today. His head was clouded by a tinderbox of contradictory emotions: He felt modest satisfaction for trapping Kaine, a serial criminal, though he was still at large; a helpless sadness that his client Jolene was becoming emotionally unraveled; and a torturous frustration at his inability to locate and capture the animal who slew Mykel. On troubled nights like this, Kyle was inconsolable.

He noticed the message light on his phone blinking, demanding attention. But tonight, he refused to listen to any more verbal flak, from *anyone*. He poured and gulped three fingers of Makers Mark before passing out in his bitterly cold bed.

CHAPTER 48

A BUCK KEY Deer, faintly illuminated, eyes glowing, posed at a far corner of her property. It was staring directly at Jo Papadapolis. A muggy breeze tried futilely to cool the night air, while heat lightning flashed across the sky revealing distant clouds layered like cast-off, unkempt sheets.

She lounged on the back deck of her mansion, midway through her third Old Fashioned. It tasted more bitter than sweet tonight. The muted splashing of her elegant, spot-lighted sea nymph fountain beyond the swimming pool, provided none of its usual comfort for her.

She periodically interrupted incoherent mumbles by throwing her head back and cackling at the full blood moon. Neither the cocktails, nor the two Valiums she'd taken earlier, dulled the fear that plagued her mind. Morbid sentiments stirred in her head, inducing a tangle of swirling, grotesque demons. *Where the hell was Dominic? And where the hell was Kyle?*

She'd already called Kyle three times and was about to dial him again when a chair leg scraped on the wooden deck behind her.

In her anesthetized state, Jolene's head lolled from side to side as she tried to turn in her seat. She fought to control her terror, realizing someone was behind her. Attempting to rise, she floundered helplessly in her chair. When she flopped back a second time, the assailant grabbed a shock of her hair and forcefully yanked on it, smashing her head onto the wooden frame of the chair back.

Horrified, Jolene's eyes flew open. Stunned and dizzy, she threw up both arms, hoping to fend off her assailant. Too late. The last thing Jolene Marie Grace Papadapolis ever saw was a crimson cloth covering her mouth and nose. She fought for both oxygen and escape. Neither the stars nor her fate permitted either this night.

CHAPTER 49

NEXT MORNING, STILL sore, but refreshed after a second cup of coffee, Kyle checked the three messages on his answering system.

"Kyle, this is Jo. I need to speak with you!"

"Kyle, please. I got…a message from Dominic… tonight. Won't be back… for another two days. I've got a b-b-bad f-f-feeling about tonight!"

"Kyle, wa' the hell. Where 'n hell…are you? I'm alone. P-P-Please call!"

The last message came through slurred, barely intelligible. It came at 10:15 last night. After trying to reach Jolene by phone, Kyle dressed and rushed out. He kept glancing at his cell phone, hoping for a new message or call from her. There were none. Pulling onto Ashley Drive, Kyle stomped on the gas pedal.

He careened onto the Papadapolis' driveway and narrowly avoided plowing into a jogger. Kyle launched from his car, and sprinted to the front door. He rang the bell and tried the knob. No one answered. He banged repeatedly on the door's frosted, etched-glass window, nearly shattering it. Still, no answer.

He dashed to the backyard. The first thing he noticed was an overturned lounge chair and side table. Through the open French doors, he saw the dining room was brightly lit. Entering, he yelled, "Jo, are you here?" No reply.

He turned around, double checking the patio to be sure he hadn't missed anything. From across the yard, Kyle realized there was something odd about the fountain. The Nymph and dolphins, her good luck charms, appeared to be shooting jets of red water. He tore across the patio, leapt onto the pool deck, and raced across the lawn to the fountain.

He pulled up short, recognizing the body of Jolene Papadapolis lying face down in the crimson-stained water of the fountain pool.

CHAPTER 50

THE TAMPA POLICE Department arrived six minutes after Kyle called 911. The medical examiner soon followed. A busy crowd of policemen had formed around the fountain while first responders moved Jolene's body onto a gurney, prepping her for transport. Three officers continued combing the patio and grounds for evidence.

A steadily falling, wind-blown shower stirred the officials to don rain gear. Kyle ignored it. He had given his statement to Sgt. Dallas and now sat on a bench off to the side, giving way to the police. Rain ran down his face, masking his mood. His hands were clasped, working each other tensely; his head was bowed.

Tony came from the front yard and offered a rain jacket to Kyle. "I figured you could use this. How you doing partner? What happened here?"

Ignoring the rainfall, he waved off the jacket. "Doing? Not so good Tony. It appears Jo was attacked and subdued on the patio and dragged to the fountain where her throat was slashed. Her body was dumped in the fountain."

"Her throat was cut? Christ, is it possible this is the work of Y2K?"

"Gotta wait for the M.E. report. Jo left me several messages last night. I didn't listen to them until this morning. Jesus Tony, when did I get so careless?"

"Woah, wait a sec Kyle. You didn't *let* this happen. The risk to her was negligible. Nothing I observed suggested *any* imminent danger to her. She suffered from a head full of morbid fears, fed by an equally unhealthy obsession with astrology."

"But, it's not my job to simply gauge the level of danger to my clients, it's to serve and protect them. Jo was in mortal fear. I let her down."

Speaking softly, almost to himself, he continued, "Damnit! I've been here before. I've let another woman die on my watch. Patrick calls it the McNally curse." He paused, head down, thinking, *A month ago, this world felt different. It was a place where good people sometimes lost and bad people sometimes won. Four weeks ago, Mykel was alive and Jolene was worried about improbable phantoms. Fuck that…it's my turn now!*

Then, out loud, "No more, Tony."

Tony smacked his fist on the bench. "Bullshit Kyle. There's no way we save 'em all. Hell, it's a good day when we get to save one. There's no telling how many women's lives we protected when we tracked and caught the Slugger. Let's drop this pity party and get to work finding Jo's killer, okay?"

"Ahh, sorry Tony. It's been a train wreck of a morning. Mykel and Jo are gone. I need to swallow that and move on."

"No problem, my friend. I get it. We'll find their killers soon enough." *You're a good man, Kyle; the closest thing to a noble man I'll ever meet.*

"I'll settle for that. For now. Let's start with motives for Jo's murder. This isn't quite Y2K's M.O., but I won't rule him out yet. Copycat? Maybe, though I'm gonna take a closer look at her husband, Dominic. He was screwing his murdered partner's wife until just over a month ago. She claims it was a fling for her. But I'm building a growing list of reasons why he'd want her husband out of the way; lust and jealousy are at the top.

"TPD confirmed his alibi for the day of Mykel and Hermann's murders. It's no coincidence that Papadapolis, Kaine, and Hermann are all tethered to the Black Dragon Security Solutions Company.

Those offices look more like a nest of vipers than a close-knit family of ex-army buddies."

A bolt of lightning, followed by an enormous crash of thunder, was instantly followed by a deluge of gully-washing rain. Kyle reached for the rain jacket from Tony.

CHAPTER 51

THE NEXT MORNING, Kyle arrived at Veronica Hermann's home at ten o'clock. Corporal O'Shea stepped out of her squad car to greet him. "Thanks for joining me, Shannon. I'd like to learn more about her relationship with Mr. Papadapolis; what she knows, and, maybe, what she suspects."

"Happy to be here, Kyle. I like Mrs. Hermann, and feel so sorry for her. Oh, I have some good news. The major told me he's got a promising lead on Kaine's location."

"That is good news. I won't be satisfied until he's behind bars. And," placing a hand over his wounded side, "I plan to be his first visitor."

AFTER BEING SEATED in the library, O'Shea said, "Mrs. Hermann, we're grateful for you agreeing to meet with us again. I know you've had a lot to deal with, given the shock of your husband's death, and now, with your friend, Mrs. Papadapolis's senseless killing. I admire your courage and honesty. We'll keep this brief."

"Thank you, corporal. I apologize for being short with you the last time you were here. These days, I struggle to manage my fear and sorrow.

I keep recalling when Felix and I were together; when we were so happy. Believe me, I'll do everything I can to help you find Felix's killer."

"Thank you, Mrs. Hermann," Kyle said. "I'm sorry, but my questions this morning deal with what I know will be sensitive, personal subjects for you. I'd like to go back to your relationship with Dominic Papadapolis."

Her head and shoulders sagged. Then, raising up with swollen, red-rimmed eyes, she said, "Although it's deeply embarrassing for me, I'll do my best to answer your questions. If I've done anything either directly or indirectly that led to Felix's death…"

Sitting beside her, O'Shea placed a comforting hand over Mrs. Hermann's.

After giving her a moment to compose herself, Kyle continued, "Please take your time. I'm sure this can't be easy. Looking back, did you ever have reason to suspect Mr. Papadapolis could be implicated in your husband's murder?"

"I spoke with Dom directly about it a couple of days after. He vehemently denied it. Of course, I'd broken off our relationship back in September; I was afraid Felix would find out. He called twice more, begging me to reconsider, though he never again tried to deny it. We'd only been together for a couple of months before I ended it.

"But, is it possible? Well, I suppose so…though he never would have done it himself. That's not his way. He always delegated. When he bought his condominium in Bradenton, he'd never even seen it. Told the realtor just to 'take care of it' for him. He liked to brag about using people. Early on, I found that brash arrogance naively appealing."

"Could you tell us where his condominium is?" asked O'Shea.

"It was in Bradenton, by the river. We once visited a museum nearby. Sorry, I don't know the address."

"Thank you, Mrs. Hermann. You've been a big help, O'Shea said.

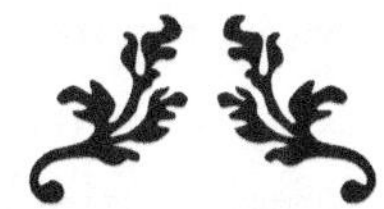

CHAPTER 52

ON THE WAY to meet with Dominic Papadapolis, Kyle called Tony. "Do me a favor. Call Patrick and Leo. I'd like to get together and review the current status of our cases. Also, do some digging on your computer. See if you can discover any holes in Dominic's alibis about his travel and layovers on his Russian trip? I'm hoping there's a problem there somewhere."

"Sure. Let's meet at Paladin. Say, five o'clock?"

"Terrific Tony. Thanks."

KYLE ENTERED THE offices of Black Dragon Security Solutions Company at 1:00 p.m.

Addressing the receptionist, he said, "Good afternoon. I'm here to speak with Mr. Papadapolis."

"I'm sorry, Mr. McNally. However, Mr. Papadapolis just returned from an overseas trip and asked not to be disturbed. May I take a message for him?"

"I'm here regarding the murder of my client, his wife. And I need to speak to him, *now.*"

"I'll check with him to confirm if he'll see you, Mr. McNally."

"I'm confident he will," Kyle said, lowering his voice, and nodding.

Moments later, entering Papadapolis' office, Kyle was surprised by the sweet, cloying scent of a flowering potted plant, branches drooping with dark purple berries, in front of the windows.

"Well, if it isn't Kyle McNally, the ill-fated gumshoe of Ybor City. I'm surprised you're here today. Shouldn't you be busy chasing down the murderer of my wife? Especially since you botched her security protection," he said, crimson color rising from his collar.

Ignoring the slight, Kyle flashed a crooked smile and said, "Glad you could squeeze me in Dom. I have a couple of problems I need help with."

"I'll give you five minutes, McNally. Unlike your agency, I've got a successful business to run here."

Without taking his eyes off Dom, Kyle strode over and stood facing the man. "Your wife's homicide is one reason I'm here."

Papadapolis began fidgeting with his fountain pen. Then, sneering, he said, "Sit down, *Mr.* McNally."

"I'm curious, Dom. How is it that of three ex-army *buddies* working in a profitable business stateside, one's been assassinated, and another is discovered to be a serial murderer? How is it possible you were oblivious to the crimes and events involving your partner and friend? Never mind that your wife, my client, was just brutally murdered three days ago while you were allegedly out of the country.

"Were you aware Scott Kaine was stalking and slaughtering homeless people in Ybor City?"

"No. Now how would I know that?"

"I spoke with his ex-girlfriend, and she tells me he struggled with PTSD and drug problems. She said his behavior became increasingly bizarre over the past several months. Weren't you concerned? Didn't you have any reason to ask him about it? Did you even notice it? He was your good friend, your army buddy, right? And now, Y2K's M.O. is all over your wife's murder."

"Listen to me, McNally, and listen closely; I didn't go home with Scott at night. We weren't buddies. I wasn't privy to his troubles or his personal demons. He was an employee and a talented computer programmer. Sure, I saw he was struggling. Felix and I spoke of it more than once, but he always did his work for me," Dom said, almost snarling.

"You're just fishing, McNally. I've got nothing to tell you about Scott, or Felix, or my wife. I don't know who shot Felix, and I don't know who murdered my wife. Her death is grievous to me. Yet, here you stand, making ridiculous claims and libelous innuendos. Why don't you get the fuck out of my office and go find real criminals?"

"Don't worry Dom, I will. You say you weren't buddies? That's not what you told me the first time we spoke about Scott. Please, take your time before answering, Dom. The Tampa police are interested too, and are currently looking into your proximity to these crimes."

Papadapolis jumped from his chair and glared at Kyle, growling, "I'll let my lawyers deal with your slanderous accusations. You're gonna pay, McNally." Then, shaking his fist at Kyle, "I swear to God, I'll close down that lousy business of yours!"

Ignoring the threat, Kyle smiled and counted to three before answering. "Veronica Hermann tells me you two were having an affair last summer. It's really no stretch to suppose that provided you with the motivation to want to push aside her husband and your wife. Lust and envy are powerful passions; headliners from the deadly sins."

With a swipe of his arm, a stack of papers flew from Dom's desk.

"Can you deny it?" Kyle shot back.

"Do you really believe I'm stupid enough to harbor a serial killer, hire an assassin, and slay my wife? Listen, whatever I did or didn't do with Mrs. Hermann is just rumor. I won't dignify *that* allegation with an answer.

Kyle stood, and with a slow smile, said, "Who said it was a hired assassin?"

"McNally, you're inferring I murdered my wife, and abetted Scott, or Y2K, or whoever in hell he was? Or maybe I helped Eddy Kaprat, the 'granny killer,' a few years back?" Papadapolis swiped with his sleeve at spittle building in the corners of his mouth.

"You know goddamn well I was out of the country when Jolene was murdered. And I don't give two flying fucks what the Tampa police are investigating! I'm guilty of none of what you're suggesting."

"I may not be able to prove it yet Dom, but I'm convinced you're involved in these murders. It was obvious from our first conversation how little respect you had for your wife. And further, it's no stretch to suppose you might be involved in Felix Hermann's murder. He was the man who stood between you and your lover, his wife. He'd also told you he was leaving Black Dragon. That kind of disloyalty must have come as quite a shock to your pride."

Looking up at his accuser with a scowl, Dom pressed the intercom button. "Olivia, call security."

Smirking, Kyle rose and walked out of Papadapolis' office.

CHAPTER 53

KYLE LEANED AGAINST the frame of an open window in the offices of Paladin Detective Agency. An earlier rainstorm had knocked out the electricity, and the air in the offices was clammy. The noise from 7th Avenue below echoed off the brick street and building walls, carrying sounds of boisterous tourists mingled with the occasional thump-thumping of motorcycles rending the air. The strong, spicey fragrance of cigar smoke, with hints of old leather and toasted nuts, snaked its way up to his office. His brooding thoughts lacked even a whisper of optimism.

By five o'clock, the lights and air conditioning were back on, though a slight aroma of stale cigar smoke still hung in the air.

Patrick came in smiling, file folders under his arm. Leo's face was impassive. Tony's eyes were downcast.

"Thanks for joining me and Tony. We've made a couple of discoveries concerning the murder of Jolene Papadapolis. Leo, we hope you'll bring us up-to-date on Scott Kaine. And, Patrick, we'd like to hear some good news concerning the whereabouts of our assassin, Dire.

"In an interview with Veronica Hermann today, I learned that Dominic Papadapolis could have a strong motive for killing his wife, Jolene. It would also explain a second crime, arranging for the assassination of his partner, her husband, Felix. It seems she and Papadapolis had an affair, which may have triggered his plan.

"Leo, your team interviewed Papadapolis concerning his whereabouts at the time of Jolene's murder." Leo nodded. "He told me your department vetted his alibi concerning his business trip to Russia. I was suspicious enough to ask Tony to check into it. Tony, were you able to find anything to dispute that alibi?"

Shaking his head, "No. My friend at the Chicago FBI confirmed what TPD found.

"Don't worry, Tony. It was a long shot.

"I met with Dominic earlier today and shared my suspicions. He didn't care much for them." Then grinning, "Not much at all. And, I'm still hoping to tie him together with Dire. Leo, you might want to call for another interview with him."

"I agree. Let me notify the station and have him brought in for further questioning." He stood and went into Tony's office to make the call.

"Patrick, any new information concerning the connections between Dominic, Scott, and Dire since we last talked?"

With a satisfied smile, he passed Kyle one of the file folders he brought and said, "That I have, son. I learned some new facts concerning Dominic Papadapolis and Axel Scott Kaine while they were stationed in Iraq. Turns out, Kaine was charged with murdering several civilians. Knife attacks, as reported. The charges were dropped early on though. His commanding officer, Mr. Papadapolis, proffered alibis claimin' the nights of the indigenes' murders, Kaine had duty with 'im. Backed it with written log reports. Smelly stuff, that. Didn't sit well with the local constabulary either."

Kyle clapped his hands and rocked back in his chair. "And I'll bet my reputation that Dominic was aware of Kaine's murderous appetites here in Ybor City too. I'm no psychologist, but Axel Scott Kaine seems to have a misanthropic hatred for the poor among us." His lips drew up into a wry smile. "And from there, it's no huge leap to imagine

Papadapolis using his knowledge to coerce Kaine into murdering his wife for him."

Kyle continued. "So far, gentlemen, this is not much more than supposition, but I believe we're closing in on Papadapolis. With the criminal Iraqi connection between him and Kaine, we have another lead concerning Jolene's murderer.

"Patrick, any updates from Interpol concerning Dire?"

"Aye. That's the second folder you'll be interested in opening. Our sniper, full name Christopher Casimir Cross, aka 'Dire', was attached by the Brits to the same unit as Lieutenant Colonel Dominic Papadapolis in Iraq. You'll find photos of him, and last known addresses in there as well. That's what you were after. Am I right?"

"Right, you are Patrick. This confirms the connections between Dominic and Mykel's murder. That bastard's been pulling the strings on all these crimes. Leo, though I'd love to be the next person Papadapolis meets today, I'll let you drop the hammer on him. I want Chris Casimir Cross, CCC.

"Leo, any updates on Kaine? O'Shea mentioned you'd gotten a lead on his location earlier."

"You bet. Kaine was apprehended at Hartsfield Airport in Atlanta earlier today. He was about to board a plane with a one-way ticket to Riyadh, Saudi Arabia. Once his arrest and identity are confirmed, we'll begin the prisoner transfer process.

"Glad to hear it; his plan makes sense. We don't have an extradition treaty with the Saudis. He was planning to disappear. He'd have connections there through his work at Black Dragon; they had several accounts he oversaw. I suspect Kaine will gladly testify about his ties to Papadapolis; it'll earn him a plea bargain with the DA."

Leo continued, "I just learned, headquarters has been unable to reach Papadapolis at home, at work, or on his cell phone.

"I'm really not surprised that Dominic's gone missing. His web of lies and deceit was collapsing," Kyle said.

CHAPTER 54

A BUZZ OF early morning excitement greeted Kyle as he walked into the Tampa Police Department at 7:30 a.m. The lingering odor of the previous night's burnt coffee invaded his sinuses painfully. When he entered Leo's office, Lieutenant Nick Willcox was already seated. He threw a disdainful scowl in Kyle's direction.

Willcox spoke first. "So, McNally, surprisingly, your initial ID of Y2K was right. I always suspected the connection between 'just ask,' and the killer's identity."

"Sorry Willcox, but you didn't know shit; never had a clue. Too late to pretend your head wasn't stuck somewhere on the wrong side of your sphincter."

"Alright gentlemen, calm down," Leo said. "Kaine has been positively identified and is right now being transported back to Tampa for arraignment." He directed a sharp glare at Willcox, the kind that sparked house fires.

"Kyle, Nick confirms that Dominic Papadapolis has gone missing. He hasn't shown up at his offices of Black Dragon Security, doesn't answer his cell phone, and no one is home at his residence."

"That confirms what I thought. Any *ideas* Willcox?" Kyle said, throwing shade his way.

"Yeah. It sounds like he realizes his world is caving in on him and he's hoping for a safe place to lie low. I found out he still has family in Greece, so I'd bet that's where he'll try to escape to. That sound about right, Leo?"

"I'm not placing any bets on overseas travel just yet, Nick. Too easy to track him with passports, credit cards, and airport security. Any other ideas, gentlemen?"

"I'm chasing a lead, but it's out of your jurisdiction. I'll keep you advised Leo, and let Willcox pursue his own *highly* intuitive ideas," Kyle said.

There was a knock on his door, followed by an officer who entered and set a folder in front of Leo. Giving it a quick scan, Leo said, "Interesting. This is the toxicology report on Jolene Papadapolis. They found a near-lethal amount of Belladonna in her blood."

Kyle sat back in his chair, shaking his head. "I'd never have guessed deadly nightshade. It induces hallucinations and delusions. That explains her erratic behavior and paranoia. She was being poisoned by Dominic."

LEAVING THE HEADQUARTERS, Kyle immediately called Tony. Tony mumbled, "Yeah, what's up Kyle?"

"Tony, meet me for coffee at the office in an hour. We've got some important work to do. I'll explain when you get there."

"Sure, boss."

Tony rolled over in bed and whispered to O'Shea, "Go back to sleep, Shannon—no need to leave. I've gotta meet Kyle. I'll call you later." He gave her an intense, tantalizing kiss and warm embrace, both instantly signaling from the south that he'd rather stay, before he slid reluctantly from their bed.

CHAPTER 55

TONY WALKED INTO Paladin Detective Agency at nine o'clock. Kyle sat at his desk, an aromatic pot of Kona coffee, just finished brewing. "Hey Tony. Thanks for meeting me here on short notice. How about a cup of coffee?"

"Love one," he said, grabbing a cup for himself.

"TPD tried contacting Dominic, but he's disappeared. He's on the run."

"You're kidding me. Why didn't he just put up a lighted billboard announcing his connection to Jo's murder?" Tony said.

Kyle grinned, and continued, "That, and his obvious connections to both Kaine's murders and Hermann's assassination. When I spoke with Veronica Hermann yesterday, she told me he owns a condominium in Bradenton. She didn't have an address, but told me it's on the Manatee River, somewhere close to a museum. I got the impression the condo was a recent purchase, a 'love nest.' Could you find that purchase and the location with your computer?"

"You bet. I'll check the online MLS listings for recent condo purchases and pull up a map to focus on the riverfront condos close to a museum."

"Excellent. I'd like to head down there as soon as you've zeroed in on his location. And, I just got back from a meeting with Leo where he learned Jolene was being poisoned with Belladonna—she wasn't just a loony astrologer."

✝ ✝ ✝

AT THREE O'CLOCK, Tony called Kyle and told him he'd located Dominic's place at the Riverside Condominiums on Point Pleasant Avenue facing the Manatee River.

"Good work Tony. I'll be by to pick you up in thirty minutes and we'll head down there."

Kyle called Leo; got his voicemail. "Leo, Tony found the location of a condo Papadapolis owns in Bradenton. We're heading out now. Not sure if Dominic's there. I'll get back to you either way."

Half an hour later they were on the road, southbound on I-275, forty-five minutes from Bradenton. Typical this time of day, traffic was snarled in St. Petersburg until they crossed the Sunshine Skyway Bridge.

When they pulled up to the Riverside Condominiums in Bradenton, Kyle told Tony to go in back of the property and secure it in case Papadapolis tried to escape that way.

Kyle walked up to the front entrance just as a resident was exiting. Responding to the resident's questioning stare, Kyle flashed his P.I. license and said, "Official business." That mollified the man. He took the elevator to the eleventh floor and stepped out, trying to locate unit eleven-thirteen.

He rang the doorbell. No answer. He rapped on the door and announced, "Dom, this is Kyle McNally. Open the door."

CHAPTER 56

DOMINIC PAPADAPOLIS SLOWLY opened the door; one arm behind his back. "You surprise me, McNally. But good. Long as you're here, c'mon in." he said, taking several steps back while raising his right hand. It held a pistol, with his finger on the trigger.

Kyle took a step in and turned to close the door. When he turned back to Dom, he ducked, spun, and drove a sweeping kick that knocked the gun from Dom's hand. It flew across the room, ending under a sofa. Kyle stood, facing the man and said, "You really don't want to do this Dom." Then bluffing, "The police are on the way."

Eyes bulging, Papadapolis screamed, "You can go fuck yourself, McNally! This is where I settle my account with you, you useless private cockroach."

He dove at Kyle, hands forming claws. Kyle deftly turned to the side and smashed Dom in the side of the head, knocking him to the floor. The man surprised Kyle by whipping over onto his back and kicking at him, landing a direct strike to the groin.

"Oof!" Buckling, Kyle groaned and staggered two steps back. He winced, took a deep breath, and readdressed his foe.

Dom regained his feet and stood, eyes aflame, chest heaving, arms raised, yelling, "There's no damn way you're gonna take me in." *I'm better than you. Always have been. Always will be!*

Dom turned and leaped, arms reaching for the sofa, hoping to recover his gun. Kyle dove after him, grabbing Dom by the ankles. He wrapped his arms around Dom's legs, restraining him; the pistol inches from his grasp.

Using his body weight to restrain his opponent, Kyle grappled his way up Dom's hips and back until he was within striking distance of his head. He pummeled him with three rapid blows to the side of the face; blood trailed from his ear. Dom was stunned, but only for a second.

Recovering with an agile move, Dom rolled over and took a swing that caught him on the back of his head, dizzying him. It was followed by a second, convulsive twist and arch, and Kyle was toppled off to the side.

Kyle shook it off. In a flash, he shot back to his knees and launched a crushing uppercut directly to Dom's chin. That one took out his lights. Papadapolis was neutralized.

Standing over Dom, Kyle called 911. He then phoned Tony. "Tony, c'mon up. I've got Dom under control. Call Leo and let him know."

CHAPTER 57

KYLE SAT ON a couch facing Papadapolis, waiting for the police to arrive. Kyle locked eyes with his captive, and said, "Dom, you were poisoning Jolene. But you got impatient; her death was taking too long. So, you gave up and arranged for her murder.

"Your revised plan included coercing Kaine into killing her. You'd gotten him out of those serial knifing jams when you two were stationed in Iraq together, so you were fully aware of his predisposition to murder. And, I'm certain you suspected his involvement in the Y2K crimes, given the M.O. He's a twisted psychopath bent on cleansing the planet of its cast out people.

Papadapolis' eyes darted back and forth between his front door and the balcony.

"I also know you coordinated the assassination of your partner, Felix Hermann. You hired a former British sniper, Cristopher Casimir Cross, to assassinate him. We traced your connection back to your time together in Iraq when, as a British sniper, he was temporarily assigned to your unit. He is now working as an assassin-for-hire here in the states. Unfortunately, and too late for Felix, Veronica told you she had no plans of staying with you. She loved her husband."

Dom shifted in his chair and said, "That's bullshit, McNally. Veronica loves me; I don't care what she told you. Sorry, but you don't know jack."

"Dom, these are facts. Kaine has been apprehended in Atlanta, and is being returned to Tampa. He'll no doubt plea bargain his way out of a date with Old Sparky. Trust me, he'll spill everything about you, how you lied to help him with those civilian murders in Iraq. That, and his insane Y2K crusade, which you surely knew about."

"Hold on McNally, you're trying to tell me I covered for a serial killer? In what universe would a man in my position be even vaguely interested in abetting a mass murderer?"

"You're not the first of your kind Dom. Not even close. I've met plenty like you in my career. You hooked Kaine when you arranged for him to escape justice overseas. That bought him an invitation into your murderous conspiracy."

Unphased, Dom stuck his chin out and said, "And this bullshit about hiring a contract killer to knock off my friend and business partner… are you serious? I loved that man!"

"Dom, you're a man who's used to getting what he wants. Like I said, I've met your kind before. You're not one who places honor and fidelity above your own selfish desires.

"Honestly, I can appreciate how you grew tired of waiting for Jolene to die from the poison you were giving her. I only wish I'd recognized that plant in your office.

"And what choice did you have? Dreading the weeks, possibly months, it might take for a slow, less conspicuous death, you took a business trip to Russia, and devised an alternate script with Kaine. It was a good plan, Dom; one that gave you a solid alibi."

Papadapolis' knees were bouncing as he said, "McNally, you're trying to pin these crimes on me because I'm a convenient scapegoat who, only coincidently, was in the vicinity of the events you describe. This is all bullshit."

"Dom, I can assure you, unless you give up Cross's location, you're gonna fry, and I'll cheer, watching you walk the green mile to your execution.

Dom exhaled, his shoulders fell, and he lowered his head.

"Dom, your world is collapsing around you. I might feel the same way in your shoes. I'm offering you a chance to reduce your exposure in this nasty mess. You tell me where Cross is, you give me his location, and I'll speak with the Tampa P.D. and the District Attorney's office on your behalf. I swear I'll do that."

Dom's gaze remained on the floor. Then, with a pinched face and a hot glare, he looked up and spat, "I still say you're full of shit McNally. You're not in a position to make me any offers."

"You're wrong, Dom. Don't forget, my friend Leo Davidson, is a major at TPD. He's a good man, a fair man. And, if you help us locate Cross, he'll be sure the D.A. hears about your assistance."

Dom's eyes closed, his chin fell to his chest, while both clenched fists dropped to his knees. He began slowly shaking his head and exhaled with a slow moan. He was broken.

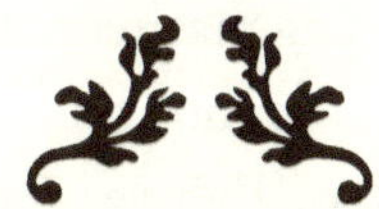

CHAPTER 58

THE BRADENTON POLICE arrived ten minutes after they were called. Dom said he never learned the name of the marina where Cross moored his large craft. However, from their conversations, he suspected it was likely one of the older ones in Sarasota County.

Kyle updated Leo, who began making the arrangements for a transfer of Papadapolis from Manatee County to Tampa.

"Tony, I need you to start a search of marinas in the Sarasota area. Look for ones more than twenty-years-old and with deep, wet slips."

"What's a wet slip?" Then, chuckling, "Sounds to me like a woman caught in a rainstorm without an umbrella."

Kyle ignored his partner's vain attempt at humor. "I'll explain later."

"I'll get started as soon as we find a local internet café. I brought my laptop computer in case we needed it."

Tony found a listing in the phone book for a nearby internet hotspot, the Binary Bean. It was after 7 p.m. when they arrived. He made the online connection, logged in, and began searching. Kyle went for two white chocolate mocha coffees with whipped cream and a couple of decadent-looking bear claws. They needed the espresso and sugar buzz.

The café bustled with hushed conversations between caffein-enlightened college kids and several small groups discussing local gossip.

The intoxicating aroma of robust coffees and sweet pastries had a energizing effect on Kyle.

Taking a cautious first sip of his steaming coffee, Kyle looked up with a white mustache and asked, "Any luck yet Tony?"

Tony chuckled, made a mocking swipe at his upper lip, and said, "Yep. I've found three promising marinas where Chris Cross could most likely to rent a slip. Moving from north to south, they are: the Sarasota Harbor Marina on Sarasota Bay. They've been in business for almost forty years. The second one, Skipper Paul's Sail Port, is in central Sarasota. This one must be high class, even has a five-star restaurant. The third one, the Luna Key Marina, is further south is on Little Sarasota Bay. It's been there since the early sixties."

Tony sat back and turned his attention to his coffee while Kyle considered their next move. "Tony, print those sites. We'll drive down to Sarasota tonight, find a motel, get some rest, and start out in the morning. We'll work the sites from north to south and see if we can coax Mr. Cross down from his masthead."

CHAPTER 59

THEY SPENT THE night at a Best Western Motel on Bee Ridge Road in west Sarasota. After a troublesome night of rumpling and kicking his sheets around, Kyle rose late Sunday morning. Tony had slept in. Shortly after breakfast, they were on the road.

While driving to their first location, the Sarasota Harbor Marina, Tony brought up a topic they'd discussed previously. "Kyle, I've given one of our first partnership conversations some consideration. You were right. Now that I'm onboard, there's no denying that our future is bright, or, as Mr. Atlas might say, irrefragable."

Kyle gave Tony a sideways glance and said, "Go on, Mr. Webster. Remind me, which conversation?"

"The one where you mentioned the possibility of hiring an office manager. With all the time we spend out of the office, and with our profits improving, it makes sense now. I've heard too many hang-ups on our voicemail. And, I'll bet some of those were from potential customers who gave up and called the next P.I. in the phone book.

"That's why I'm thinking it's important to hire someone who could answer those calls and get them to us promptly. Not to mention the advantages of keeping better office records and accounts. So, how do you feel about it today?"

Kyle gave Tony an attentive nod. "I've thought more about it too, but I have no idea how we'd find someone. They would need to be smart, well organized, and personable. Do you have someone in mind?"

"I do, though it isn't my idea. Shannon suggested we ask Rosalina if she'd be interested. She has the right personality for the position. She's a capable customer service worker; she's intelligent, loyal, dependable, and cares deeply about the staff she manages at the cantina. Those qualities are difficult to assess from people responding to help wanted ads. Shannon also learned she'd worked as a secretary and bookkeeper at the offices of the Ministry of Education before leaving Cuba. What do you think?"

"I'm not against it, but right now, what I think is we're nearing the end of an important case, and I have to stay focused. You're aware how much this one means to me. Capturing Cross may help to ease my conscience, but until he's either dead or behind bars, I won't be sleeping peacefully."

Then, following a brief hesitation, Kyle said, "Okay, you're right. But let's put a pin in it for now and go get Chris Cross."

"Roger that, partner."

THEIR FIRST DESTINATION was at the Sarasota Harbor Marina. Tony read the advertisement he'd printed from their web site, "Easy access to Gulf of Mexico. What they call 'wet slips' accommodate up to seventy-foot boats. Rentals on a first-come, first-served basis. They've even got a tiki bar with food service."

Kyle knew about slip rentals and marina services from the Floribbean Flow deck boat he and Mykel owned. "Most full-service marinas offer both dry storage and wet slips, plus other amenities. The dry storage is for longer term or occasional use storage, and the wet slips are intended for convenient, on-the-water access, or people who live on their boats."

Kyle parked in the lot directly in front of the marina's office. It was Sunday, so he wasn't sure they'd find the manager in.

On entering the office, they were greeted by a young, attractive, indigo-haired woman standing behind the counter. She was above six-feet tall, had stunning emerald eyes, wore an orange scarf with pewter and black flags knotted into a skull cap, and had on a figure flattering laced leather vest. She gave them a welcoming smile accompanied by a roguish wink and said, "Ahoy there, mates. I'm Trixie, Trixie Page, the weekend first mate here. How may I get you to shake loose some of your plunder today?"

Tony did a double take, imagining they'd mistakenly walked into the property's tavern. Kyle approached the counter, smiled and said, "Sorry Trixie, but you'll get none of our booty today. At least not for anything in your slips or on your shelves. But I've got no objection to paying for information."

"Well, if it doesn't involve treasure maps or sunken ships, I'll try to help you, Mr.—"

"McNally, Kyle McNally, and this is my partner, Tony Petrocelli," he said, showing his P.I. license.

"Pleased to meet you Mr. McNally," she said, while directing a mile-wide, tooth-filled grin at Tony. "And you too, Tony P."

"Trixie, we're trying to find a man whose wife suggested he might be docked here on their sail boat. She told me he left her without a word. She's worried, and hired us to find him," Kyle said.

Trixie scratched her head and pursed her lips before saying, "We don't get many missing buccaneers here. This runaway, he gotta name?"

"Christopher Cross. Mrs. Cross says he's been gone more than a week and the police in Hillsborough County haven't got a clue. He's a part-time sailor, and took off on their forty-five-foot schooner. We're taking a chance he may be holed up here, possibly with Mrs. Cross's best friend."

"Oh, that kind of pirate, huh?" Trixie winked, flashing another smile at Tony as she scanned their rentals and shook her head. "Name doesn't ring a bell, and there's no one in our books renting by that name. You gotta picture?"

Kyle pulled the two photos Patrick had given him from Interpol. One, a British Army photo, the second one, taken of him with a beard, shortly after his separation. Trixie studied both pictures for a moment and shook her head. "Sorry, Mr. McNally, no one here resembles this fella. I'd like to help you." And with a twinkle in her eye, "And *you*, Tony P."

Kyle nodded and placed a fifty on the table. "Thank you, Trixie."

Tony walked out, mimicking a tip of the hat and a wink to Trixie. Her eyes lingered on him all the way to their car.

IT WAS ALREADY two-thirty when Kyle pulled into a parking space at Skipper Paul's Sail Port. There were several limousines—engines running, chauffeurs waiting—in the lot and a jacketed valet lazily leaning on the podium in front of the covered walkway to the entrance of the restaurant, *Chez Pierre*. The sign on the door read, "Members Only."

"Jeezus," Tony said. "This makes the last marina seem like a ghetto."

"And, we're not going to be eating dinner here tonight. Our travel budget is about two stars lower. Come on, let's try to find an on-site manager."

On crossing the lot to the office, Kyle was taken by the beautifully landscaped grounds. Christmas Palms lined the waterfront, with thick beds of Sea Ox-eye checker-boarded with Beach Morning Glories between. Kyle sarcastically said to Tony, "This outfit must pay mucho dinero to maintain these gardens."

"This is a marina? I was sure you accidentally drove us onto the grounds of Ringling's Ca' d'Zan home. This is miles beyond any hedge work I saw around Chicago, done by the *Tree Fellers*."

The sign on the office door had an optimistic "Manager will return at" sign with clock hands, showing they *might* be back by four o'clock. It was just two-thirty now. Kyle said, "Let's head back to that burger shack we passed a couple miles back."

"A cold brew sounds good to me," Tony said.

At four o'clock, fueled by sandwiches and cold beers, they waited on a bench in front of the marina offices. Twenty minutes later, Tony said, "The marina business here must operate on a different time zone than the Chez Pierre."

A tall, gangly man with unruly hair and a full, rust-gone-to-gray beard, wearing a beat-up captain's hat, came around the corner of the building. He walked past the two without a glance in their direction, unlocked the door without saying a word, and stepped inside. He took down the sign in the window and leaned back out, saying, "Hep you two?" before turning back in and taking up his director's chair post behind the counter. Stepping inside, Kyle took in the enormous array of fishing tackle, lures, nets, maps and guides, informational posters, caps, t-shirts, and a smattering of customer photos. Bait tanks lined two side walls.

This was Tony's first visit to a bait shop. On entering, he almost retched at the putrid odors assaulting his nose, including live bait, rancid salt water, and what he could only imagine was fish shit. He'd also noticed a repugnant metallic taste forming in the back of his throat. He seriously considered stepping back outside to wait for Kyle.

Kyle said, "Hello, I'm hoping to speak with the manager." Ignoring him, the old salt pulled out a delicately carved Meerschaum pipe, carefully stuffed it with a sweetly aromatic tobacco he dug from within a shabby gray leather pouch. He regarded Kyle from beneath hooded eyes, struck a match, and puffed his pipe to life before answering.

"You found 'im. Skipper Paul's the name."

Kyle showed his P.I. license and said, "I'm a private investigator and I've been asked to help find a friend of ours. His wife reported him missing a couple of weeks ago and the police haven't had any luck locating him. I told her I'd try to find him."

"That's not sump'in falls under my job description."

"I understand, sir…"

"Ain't no *sirs* at this port, so you best leave go of that title."

"Fine. But please, let me show you a couple pictures of this man, a Mr. Christopher Cross," placing them on the counter before the old salt.

Blowing a smoke ring directly in Kyle's face, the man chuckled and said, "Chris Cross? Now there's a name worth stowing in your money pouch. Too bad though; can't say as I recognize the name or seen this fellow ported here."

"Are you sure?" while pulling a fifty-dollar bill from his wallet and setting it down on the counter.

"See here young fella, you don't need to go wavin' money at me to get the truth—I'm an honest sailor who don't take kindly to bribes or lies. So, if you're tellin' me the truth, I'm givin' you the truth back for free. Not a familiar name, and never came across this face before," he said, pointing at the photos with the tip of his pipe. "And, if that's all you came for, I'd say this'd be a damn good time for you to say goodbye."

Kyle put the money back in his wallet and said, "Sorry for the trouble, Skipper," and turned to leave. Tony was already waiting outside.

"Weird. That was like stepping onto the deck of the Pequod to visit Captain Ahab, right?" Tony said.

Frowning, Kyle said, "Let's go. I'd like to make it to Luna Key Marina before they close."

CHAPTER 60

I T WAS FIVE-THIRTY, and the sun was setting by the time they arrived at Luna Key Marina, south of Sarasota. A sign on the office door showed they'd arrived thirty minutes after closing. Across the parking lot stood a restaurant encircled by moss-draped live oaks and a gigantic silver fiberglass grouper swinging from chains beneath the sign. The rusted chains creaked in a soft breeze. Kyle suggested they stop in for a meal before finding a motel for the night.

On entering the eatery, the smell of the outside salty air was replaced by the inviting aromas of briny fresh seafood, deep-fried hush puppies, garlic, lemon, wood, and smoke.

"Damn," Tony said. "I'm already drooling."

They sat by a window overlooking Little Sarasota Bay. The western sky delivered reflections of honey-gold and scarlet, flaring between stark silhouettes of coconut palms lining the shore.

The waitress stopped by to drop off menus and take their drink orders. When the drinks arrived, Kyle raised his glass of Maker's Mark and said, "Well Tony, we're down to the last of our three likely marinas. Here's hoping we catch a break and find Cross here."

Tony tipped his bottle of Yuengling to Kyle, "Amen. I've gotta say, I'm feeling lucky tonight, Kyle."

The young, willowy waitress returned for their food orders. Standing beside Kyle, and just a skosh taller than his head, she possessed a cheery, vivacious smile, obviously meant to capture Tony's attention. "I'm Lydia. What would you gentlemen like to order this evening?"

Kyle asked, "Hello Lydia. Let me ask, what would you recommend?"

"One of my favorites on the menu is the lobster roll. It's a sandwich. Our cook serves one of the best in Sarasota County. That, and a side of hush puppies will put a smile on your face and leave a grateful spot in your bellies. I'd also recommend his she-crab soup to start. If you've never tried it before, it's an excellent one with a combination of heavy cream, Atlantic Blue Crab meat, his own blend of mace-based seasoning, and a splash of dry sherry to give it a little snap."

Tony put down his menu and said, "Lydia, say no more. I'll have them all. That'll be three firsts for me."

Her cheeks reddened slightly, and her eyelashes lowered to half-mast as she replied, "You won't regret it."

Kyle said, "Thanks. Same for me tonight, Lydia."

After she'd gone to place their order, Kyle said, "I don't know how you do it, but you have a curiously magnetic appeal with women." Then, nodding slightly and grinning, "I'm doubt she even realized there were two of us at the table."

"Well, one thing I've noticed, Florida women take to me more than those from the windy city. Maybe it's a southern thing. That said though, I'm a one-woman man. Shannon O'Shea has my full attention these days."

"Then she's a lucky woman and you're a fortunate man."

During their meal, the sky had noticeably darkened and lightning strikes flashed out over the water. After finishing, Lydia asked if they would like dessert. Kyle said, "Thanks, not tonight, Lydia. Bring me the check. But, may I ask you a question?"

"Sure."

"We came here hoping to meet with the marina's Harbor Master. We're trying to find a friend whose wife tells us he's gone missing," then, glancing around at nearby tables, "and frankly, she's worried he may be shacking up with her best friend. He's a part-time sailor, and she believes he may be berthed at one of the area marinas."

Lydia hesitated for a moment, then directing a smile at Tony said, "Well then, you're in luck, mister. The Skipper came in just after you did. That's him at the bar," she said, pointing the man out to Kyle. He was a wizened old fella with long silver hair braided into a pony tail. He spoke with a middle-age bartender at the upper limit of her prime years, as she leaned seductively over the bar, giving him a view few men would turn away from.

Kyle thanked her as he and Tony walked over and sat beside the man. Kyle asked what he was drinking and ordered three Yuengling drafts.

"You wanna tell me why you're buying my beer mister? Since we never met, I'd guess that you're either gay, or are about to ask me a question. And, since the two of you don't appear like you bat from the other side of the plate, I'm gonna assume you want something else."

Kyle showed his P.I. license and handed him a business card. "Yes, that's right. I'm Kyle McNally, and this is my partner, Tony Petrocelli. We operate a detective agency out of Tampa. We're here searching for a man whose wife asked us to help find him. The wife suspects he may have sailed here, and is diddling her best friend."

"Nice to meet you, Kyle. Sad to hear about the man's troubles, but it's the ages-old biblical sin of infidelity. Common enough among men like me who make their living over the water. I've been told many of these stories over the years by men spilling salt water in their beers. Yep, many a weak man succumbs to that lusty bait," he said, and sighed.

A powerful gust of wind pushed hard against the windows, accompanied by a burst of lightning brilliantly exposing every shadow in the room. Not a second later, a tremendous detonation of thunder shook the building. "Weather's taking a wicked turn out there," he added sardonically.

Kyle nodded and shrugged, "Sure is. I hope it'll hold off until we can find a hotel. But, do me a favor and take a look at a couple photos of the man we're trying to find. Be nice if you recognized him. I'd love to be able to tell his wife we found him." Then with a smirk, "And, if he's alone, I'll tell her to call off the lawyers."

"Sure. Why not? Order another draft if you'd be so kind and I'll take a look-see."

Tony ordered another round while Kyle placed the two photos in front of the man.

"This fella? Sure, I know 'im. His boat's been docked in slip forty-three for the past couple months. You gotta name?"

"Mrs. Cross says his name is Christopher, last name Cross. Is that the name in your records?"

"Nope. The identification he registered with says his name is Morgan Pendragon. His boat is a classy fifty-four-foot Irwin. And it's loaded, got two guest cabins, and an elegant V.I.P. stateroom. A real gem I'll say. Name on the vessel is *Dyer Fate*. Don't see too much of him myself. He stops by here one or two days a week. Always pays his slip fees on time. None of his neighbors claim he's the gregarious type, but for me, that's no concern. Long as he drops off his rent on time, I'm good."

"You say he's ported in slip forty-three?"

"That's right."

"Is he aboard today?"

"He was yesterday. Can't say as I'm sure he stayed over though."

"Will access be a problem? I'd like to meet without spooking him. According to his wife, this isn't the first time he's taken off on one of his peccadillos."

"You make sure there's no problems. I won't stand for no trouble here."

"No, no. Don't worry. That's not gonna happen Skipper. I've handled these domestic cases discreetly before."

"Well then, if you can keep a secret, our security gate has been offline for over a week. I've been told by my electrical *wizard* he'll have it fixed any day now..." he said, with a cynical shake of his head.

Another ominous blast of lightning and a building-shuddering crack of thunder reminded Kyle it was time for he and Tony to find shelter for the night.

A FULL-BLOWN SQUALL had passed over by the time the two men settled into their hotel room. They discussed a plan for approaching Cross's boat in the morning. They agreed they should arrive before dawn, hoping they'd find him still sleeping.

At six-thirty in the morning, both men walked through the entry gate to the Luna Key Marina. They made their way through the rows of docked boats, searching for slip forty-three. The night's storms had broken, but a dense morning fog hadn't lifted yet. Tony inhaled the sickly odor of salt air rising from the water. To him, it smelled like an open Chicago sewer.

Both had their holstered Sig Sauers ready, safety's off. The plan was to have Tony walked casually past the boat, checking for any signs that Cross was on board. Kyle stood back, waiting for his signal. Then, Tony would provide backup, placing Cross between them while Kyle approached *Dyer Fate*.

"Be alert, Tony, Cross may be waiting for us."

They found the boat in the middle of a three-hundred-foot pier. Tony walked ahead, and ten steps past the bow, he stopped and turned to signal. At that moment, through a thinning fog, Kyle recognized a figure stepping onto the cockpit. He also realized that from his angle, Tony didn't see him or suspect what was about to happen.

Before he was able to alert Tony to the danger, Kyle saw the shadowy figure raise an arm and heard the crack of a pistol shot. Tony fell to the pier. Kyle raced across the twenty feet to the boat in seconds and came within six feet of the stern before diving at Cross and landing with both arms wrapped around the man. Both fell. Cross's gun spun across the deck and ended against the starboard wall.

Cross, attempting to free himself, angled a powerful sweep of his right elbow at Kyle, but only managed a glancing blow off the shoulder. The momentum of the attempt forced Kyle off him. Both men sprang to their feet, panting.

"Well well, Kyle McNally." Then, with a sneer, "I've been expecting you. What took you so long? Dom told me you were a proper sleuth; not likely. How'd it take you this long to find me? A *good* copper could have been here a week ago.

"Once I'm through with you, I'll dispense with your clumsy partner."

"Sorry Cross, you're not going to fulfill either of those wishes. I'm here to make sure you rest in peace. So, save the bold talk for the writing on your epitaph."

With a swift move, displaying the speed of a black belt, Cross spun left and uncocked his right leg head-high at Kyle. Kyle leapt back to avoid the kick. Cross landed solidly on both feet; two feet closer to his pistol.

"Still mad that I off'd your girlfriend? he said, sneering. "From what I saw, she was no great looker anyway."

Kyle growled. He feinted with a move to the left, crouched, and came up with both fists clenched, landing two quick jabs to Cross's ribs. Cross stumbled back, holding his side and coughing.

"Fuck you Dire. You're not as clever as your British Army medals made you appear. Killing Mykel was a mortal mistake. Shooting my partner will be your last mistake."

With that, Kyle took a quick step left, attempting to land a round-house hook on Cross. It didn't land as Cross bent to dodge it. He unfolded and threw a quick left jab back at Kyle's side. The blow landed punishingly on Kyle's right ribs. Cross pressed on with another jab at Kyle's left side. It landed and produced a howl from Kyle. He doubled over from the mind-numbing pain inflicted to his re-dressed knife wound.

In a second, he straightened and drew a deep breath. *Don't quit now McNally!* With blazing eyes he yelled, "Is that the best you got, Dire? Cuz' it ain't good enough! Not nearly good enough!" he said, drawing his pistol from its holster.

Cross turned, intending to retrieve his gun. With clenched teeth, Kyle yelled, "Stop, or I swear to God, I'll shoot," aiming his pistol at Cross's head.

Cross hesitated only an instant before desperately lunging to recover his weapon.

Kyle gave him an extra half-second before putting a bullet in his right leg. *Pop!*

"That one's just to remind you I'm still here *Cross*."

Cross groaned and instinctively covered the wound with both hands. He should have left them there.

The moment Kyle saw him reach with his other hand to grab the pistol, *Pop!* Kyle dropped another bullet in his left leg.

"And *Dire*, she wasn't my girlfriend, she was my fiancée." With that, Kyle leveled his aim at Cross's head. Shrugging, Cross raised both hands while sarcastically attempting to mimic the face of someone who cared. Kyle lowered his aim and shot the man quickly three times. *Pop, Pop, Pop!* All hit their mark; the first two in the palm of his right, shooting hand, and the third shattered the same wrist. He'd never pull a trigger again.

CHAPTER 61

LEAVING CROSS MOANING and clutching his now-useless, bloody right hand, Kyle jumped over the boat's gunwale and in two long strides, was crouching beside Tony, who struggled awkwardly to hold both hands over his left side, one anterior and one posterior. "How're you doing Tony?"

"I think I'll be alright…but I'm gonna need something to stop the bleeding. Blood's red, not black. That's good, right?"

"Right." Kyle ran back for the boat's first aid kit and returned. Kneeling beside Tony, he treated and covered the wounds, both entry and exit, and wrapped Tony in a mile of gauze.

"Did you do it, partner? I heard five shots. Did you kill him?"

"Nah. Though I *literally* disarmed him," Kyle said, grinning.

"How'zat?

"After dropping a round in each of his legs, I put two more bullets through his gun hand, and a third one that shattered the wrist. He'll never be able to pull a trigger or clench that fist again."

"God damn, Kyle, I'm proud of you. And, Mykel would be too."

Kyle called 911 before walking back to scrape up Cross. He called Leo. "Leo, I got him."

"Will he be standing for his arraignment?"

"No, he'll be in a wheelchair. Push to shove, Leo, it's what Mykel would have wanted me to do."

Kyle stepped back on the pier just as the sun broke through the fog. He dropped to one knee on the dock, and whispered words of gratitude for avenging his lost mate.

CHAPTER 62

THREE DAYS LATER, and two weeks before Christmas, Kyle and Tony were seated in the Guadalupe room at the Sagua La Grande Cantina. Both of them had side wounds that were stitched, wrapped, and on the mend. It was after closing, and both Guillermo and Rosa had joined them.

A toast by Guillermo was offered. Flashing a broad smile, he said, "To the brave and honorable men who protect our Ybor City. We are grateful." Then, more seriously, "And, for having avenged the murder of my friend Queasy, I am forever in your debt." They all toasted.

Raising his glass, Tony halted, crying, "Damn, my side hurts like crazy."

"Quit your whining, Tony. It's barely more than a flesh wound," Kyle said with a mischievous grin.

"What! I beg your pardon…it went clean through from front to back," Tony corrected, feigning indignation.

Rosa interjected, "Now, now, Kyle. Tony earned this time of self-pity. From what he tells me, he took a bullet for you."

Chuckling, Kyle responded, "Took a what for who? Next time, Tony, duck!"

All broke into raucous laughter as Guillermo called for the dining room manager to bring another round of drinks.

"So Tony, do you have plans for the Christmas holidays," Rosa asked.

"I'm heading home to Chicago to visit my family. Shannon is coming with me. They want to meet her."

"Well, that sounds like there's something more serious between you two."

"I won't say no, Rosa. What about you? Have you made any plans?" Tony said.

"Yes. Guillermo and I are going to close the restaurant for a few days and travel to Miami where we have several families of cousins, nieces, and nephews. We've been so busy here at the La Segunda, we haven't been with them in several years." Then raising her eyebrows and nodding at Kyle, "And what about you? Are you doing anything special for the holidays?"

"No. Nothing special. Leo and Camille have invited me over for a Christmas Eve dinner, but the rest of the holidays, I'll be staying close to the Paladin offices. I'll Likely get together with Patrick for drinks."

Guillermo excused himself, apologizing that he needed to finish closing the cantina. "Rosa, please remain with our friends. I'll be back."

After Guillermo left the room, Kyle scooted his chair closer to the table and said, "Rosa, Tony and I have been talking about something that we hope may interest you. The Paladin Detective Agency is growing beyond our ability to keep up with the day-to-day details of running a business. We both agree it's time to hire a manager, one who could keep up with client contacts, scheduling, and bookkeeping.

"With your experience in office management while you worked for the Cuban Ministry, we believe you'd be a perfect fit for us. I'm prepared to offer you a sizeable starting salary, including a generous benefit package. As the business grows, you could count on regular raises."

Tony jumped in, "Actually Rosa, it was Shannon who suggested you. She believes you would add a professional air to the business. You have great customer service skills, and first-rate problem-solving instincts. Combined with your business experience, we couldn't find a more qualified candidate."

"So, what do you think of the offer, Rosa?" Kyle asked. "I'll understand if you decide not to accept; I know you have many responsibilities here at Sagua La Grande, and I also respect your family commitment to your brother, Guillermo."

Rosa blushed before answering. "Kyle, Tony, this is quite unexpected. I'm very flattered that you'd consider me for this position. It's attractive, I must say. But, please give me a little time to consider it. As you can imagine, I'll need to speak with Guillermo about it. He's not just my brother, but also my best friend and trusted counselor."

"Absolutely, Rosa. Please consider it, and talk it over with Guillermo. I'll be happy to wait until after the holidays for your answer. In the meantime, I'll outline the full details of my offer."

CHAPTER 63

ON A CHILLY Christmas morning, Kyle took the *Floribbean Flow* out on Tampa Bay. Chopin's Nocturne in C# was sweetly playing on the radio. As the dawning sun crested over the horizon, its illumination airbrushed streaks of stratus clouds resembling giant golden feathers. The gentle, breeze-driven rolling of the boat usually comforted him, but today he sat in the cockpit, hands clenched on the helm, head bowed, tears welling in his eyes. He recalled the words from the horoscope Jolene gave him: '*…a man of honor who, unfortunately, lives in a world which cares little for such virtues.*' Today, with his aching heart, he lived with a dimmer sun, a paler sky above, and a darker sea beneath him. He was a man alone, and the world offers little solace for the lonely.

EPILOGUE

A NEW YEAR'S Day gathering was underway at Kyle's condominium. Tony and Shannon arrived early to decorate with seasonal decor. Rosa and Guillermo provided a gourmet Cuban feast with Ropa Viega, Shrimp Creole, and red beans with rice. Leo and Camille provided cognac-imbued brownie truffles for dessert. Patrick provided the spirits. The air was filled with aromas of butter, garlic, paprika, and intoxicating Grand Marnier-laced sweets. Mozart's melancholic String Quintet No. 4 played quietly beneath the conversations.

Drinks were mixed and poured by Patrick, who then announced, "May I propose a toast?" All raised their glasses as he continued, "We joyfully come together here with friends and family. I remember an adage my father loved. I'll share it now for the one whose passing leaves behind both great joy at having known her beautiful heart, and our immense sorrow at her passing, *If there ever comes a day where we can't be together, keep me in your heart. I'll stay there forever.'* for our dear Mykel. May she rest in peace."

Glasses were tipped, and more than a few tears shed. When Kyle spoke, he said, "Last week I stumbled across an anonymous poem I've kept for years. It always touched me deeply. Mykel loved its implicit Buddhist sentiment.

In The Hours Between 12:00am and Midnight
Inhale, I am here,
Exhale, I am gone,
Inhale, you're still here, so smile!"

"Hear, hear," Patrick said. "Smile we will, though our hearts break for her loss, they swell with her memory."

THE SPIRITS OF the diners had lifted, the meals and desserts had been enjoyed, when Rosa and Guillermo stood to address their friends. Rosa spoke first. "Friends, I have an announcement I'd like to share with you all. Several weeks ago, Kyle asked me to consider joining him and Tony at the Paladin Detective Agency as their Office Manager. After considering it, and speaking with my brother about it, I've decided that yes, I would love to accept his offer. Oh, and the pay ain't bad either," she said, with an appreciative nod to Kyle. All applauded vigorously; none with more enthusiasm than Kyle and Tony.

Guillermo said, "Kyle and Tony, I am sad to have Rosalina leave the cantina. But, for any other work, or any other company, I would not approve it. But with you two Hermanos, I could not say no to her. I'm happy for all three of you, and pray for much good fortune."

THE NEXT DAY, Kyle and Tony were busy at the agency discussing the arrangements for Rosa's arrival. Furniture and carpeting would need to be ordered for her reception area. They'd also reviewed the accounts to confirm all were current and correct. The phone rang on Kyle's desk and he answered.

"Hello. Yes, this is Kyle McNally. Who? Commander Rouse? Sure,

I'll speak with him." Kyle covered the mouthpiece and said to Tony, "Hey Tony, it's Rouse. W-T-F?" Then, "Al, I'm surprised to hear from you…what do you want?…Yes, Tony's down here at the agency and we're doing well…so, did you need something?…no, no I haven't been following Chicago news, why?…What did you say?…he escaped? You're kidding, right?…when did this happen?…a week ago…he did what?… and he's heading south?…and you're just calling me now?…send me what you've got…yes, I'm grateful Rouse…sure…keep me updated, okay?… Oh, and notify Leo Davidson here at the Tampa P.D.…yeah, he's a major here….okay, Rouse." Kyle placed the receiver back in the cradle and gave Tony a grim stare.

"Tony, Francis Butler, our *Slugger*, escaped from Chicago-Read Hospital for the criminally insane last week. Rouse tells me they found documents hidden in his cell indicating he may be heading to Florida. But before he left town, he stopped long enough to savagely torture and kill his aunt, Helen Butler."

NOT THE END YET!

ABOUT THE AUTHOR

J. E. Boydston, a retired Professor Emeritus, has an extensive background in education and publishing. He authored a popular annual reference guide for school personnel in the U.S. while serving as the Technical Manager and Consultant in a central Florida school district. He also served fifteen years as a Professor of Networking Technologies  for South Florida State College. A Vietnam Veteran, he earned a Purple Heart and a Bronze Star for valor during his tour. With two loving children, a brilliant granddaughter, and his first grandson due in the spring of 2025, he's a very happy writer! Boydston continues to work on the Kyle McNally detective series with his co-author and sister, M. Brooke McCullough.